A Tale of The Feyra
Tale 3

Dee

And The People

George R. Mead

E-Cat Worlds Press

This is a work of fiction. All the characters and events portrayed are creations of the imagination, nothing more, nothing less.
Comments and questions? –> gmead01@gmail.com

Dee and The People

LCCN 2012900880

Mead, George R.
Dee and The People /
George R. Mead.
p. cm. – Dee and The People (A Tale Of The Feyra; Tale 3)
ISBN-13 978-0-9817446-8-1
1. Fantasy. I. Title. II. Series.

E-Cat Worlds established its publishing program as a reaction to the large commercial publishing houses currently dominating the book industry and the smaller intellectual clones. It is interested in publishing works of fiction and non-fiction that are often deemed insufficiently profitable or commercial or that are not necessarily reflective of literary trends and fads.

E-Cat Worlds, 57744 Foothill Road, La Grande OR 97850
www.ecatworldspress.com
SAN 255-6383

In the middle of nowhere - Creativity.

First Edition:
Printed in the United States of America

From Grandeville.

Portal
Lair
Search
Not Again
And Again.
Magiwitch
Rebirth
Offspring
Holiday
Treasure
E'Nilt
Braidna

A Tale of The Feyra

Jonathon and Dee
Dee Of The Fontala
Dee and The People

Nonfiction

A History of Union County
The Ethnobotany of the California Indians
A History of The Chinese in The West: 1848-1880

Somewhere. Written in A Thin Volume.

Once upon a time in the ever so long ago past.
It happened.
A wise man saw an angel.
Or some members of his tribe so said.
Not so, he told them, slowly, sagely, shaking his head.
It was true, he stated. Great white wings.
Not so, he told them carefully.
Not an angel.
It was a demon.
Some of his tribe argued against this.
Angels do not wear dark clothes, he cried into
their arguments.
Angel's garments glow with white light.
He walked away, into the desert, slowly shaking his head.
Abandoning those who would create false tales.
It did no good.

A New Daughter

Maryland.

"I have a piece of good news," said Charles, the largest person in the room, as he refilled his beer mug. He was really happy. Good news, for them, was quite hard to come by. He was beaming.

"Oh?" Ralph smiled at him across the table top. Ralph was the smallest man in the room, a good head and a half shorter than Charles.

The six of them, three couples, The Council as they had named their group, using a name that signified nothing, had finished dinner and were now relaxing over dessert and sipping at their favorite beverage in Ralph's dining room. It was large enough to handle three couples and a few guests.

The dining room was paneled in dark wood with wide molding. The thick rug was a deep burgundy. The variable lighting in the room was set at a level pleasing to the eyes. The chairs set around the polished wood table were comfortable with plush cushions and backs. All in all, it was a very relaxing room for lovely meals, delicious desserts, and very nice after dinner libations.

They were a very special and a very privileged and a very unknown group, other than by name, that was a part of the complexity of national security.

Ralph was the Director of The Council and the only one known to his boss, the President of The United States. Their charter kept them in existence regardless of who or what party happened to temporarily occupy the White House.

Each of the other five swung great weight and authority within their respective organizations. While Ralph was known, face to face, with the President, the others were merely shadows unknown. Their charter was quite specific. The Council was given those rare and serious problems that were difficult to solve, that is, they were given to Ralph and he decided whether they would solve them as well as the manner, the methods, and the timing, if they did it. It was totally up to The Council to work in whatever way they deemed appropriate. They could not be questioned, they could not be second-guessed, they could not be de-funded. Given these parameters, they all were very serious about their job.

They were meeting in the home of Ralph and Sandra. Their house looked, more or less, like all the other houses in this area of moderately-sized, moderately priced houses. The neighbors thought that Ralph and Sandra were a nice couple, quiet and well mannered, who often had a few friends over for dinner.

No one, other than the six people concerned, knew that this house, during its extensive remodeling, had become unlike any other house in the area.

No sound could escape the house, either human or electronic. No ears, either human or electronic, could hear anything that happened inside the house including telephone conversations or any other device currently residing there.

The grass was neatly trimmed, the house was always well maintained.

All in all, it was just one house among all the others with neatly trimmed lawns and well maintained exteriors.

The homes of Charles and Prentice, and, Randy and Anabelle had the same features as this house. It came with the job.

So, Ralph smiled at his *Number Two*, took a swallow from his wine glass, and said, "Oh?" It was good to see Charles happy about some sort of news.

The rest waited. The always waited on the other, whoever it might be.

"I," stated Charles, "have heard from a little bird inside that ever so closed, ever so secure, and ever so secret research facility that got their hands on our analysis of those cut edges that did all that destruction at William Williams the Third's research facility."

"And?" prompted Ralph.

Charles grinned. "They gave up. None of that bunch could figure it out." He topped up his mug and shook a few grains of salt into the thick white foam that capped his beverage.

Randy nodded before taking a sip from his very old Brandy. Then he looked over at Ralph. "Any new business?"

Ralph shook his head. "Nope. For this group the world is calm and quiet." He smiled at them. "Maybe we all ought to take a vacation while we have the chance? Before some other news turns up."

Charles laughed. "Good idea! How long?"

"Let's plan on a month or so," said Ralph. "Unless something comes up."

They sat for a while longer and then headed for their respective homes, to plan their vacations, a few and far between occurrence. For them.

House Mataraen.

The perfectly square room was plain with undecorated walls. The furnishings were carved wood and were just comfortable enough. The lamp overhead cast a circle of illumination onto the table top, not too bright, not too dim.

They sat at the small table and sipped from their cups, large, heavy cups.

Zarten nodded and set down his cup.

"There is a delicate, ah ummmmm, task I would have you do."

Kanatar nodded and took a sip.

Zarten told him, in detail, and why.

Kanatar gasped and was glowered at.

He nodded. "As the House Head wishes." Setting his cup down, he stood and walked from the room. He would have to be careful, cautious.

House Darthar Na.

Dee sat in one of the small comfortable rooms with a large outside window that framed the view of the forest and the large meadow at the base of the entry stairs. The chairs in this room were curved gently to hold the occupant in a warm embrace.

She held a large cup of coffee in one hand, taking a small sip now and then as her mind wandered. Sprawling on her side in front of Dee was Purr Cat, one of The Furleen, a large lion-sized cougar-looking feline, acting as a handy foot stool for Dee's bare toes to wiggle in the thick fur.

Dee took another sip and smiled to herself. It was a smile of amazement. Her life had certainly changed during the not very long ago. It had been not a small change, but a large and still ongoing change. Her life changes including having two, unplanned daughters.

All of her memories were of having been raised by her parents as a normal but talented child who knew herself as Dee Grant.

As a young woman she had begun to write and not all that much time later she became a moderately well known and a moderately successful author whose name appeared on the dust jackets of her novels as D. Grant.

As an author she had been on a number book tours here and there across the United States, giving readings, signing copies of her books, and doing all the other things that an author got stuck doing. She was always accompanied by her friend and assistant, Janice.

It was on one of these book tours that Dee had learned that her home had burned to the ground and that both her parents had died in that fire.

Some time later she walked from her new home, bought from her inheritance and earnings, one of the widely scattered and rather isolated houses built on a high cliff overlooking the Pacific Ocean, and strolled over to talk with her neighbor, Jonathon, about a problem that she was having.

Since then her life had changed in ways she could never have anticipated as Jonathon helped her with that problem.

During the process of solving that problem she had learned that she wasn't really like any of those people that she had grown up among, Homo sapiens sapiens. She was one of The Feyra, a line of beings that had split millions of years in the very long ago from the people line of development and had become something quite different. Then, in a great surprise to her, she had learned that all of her memories of being raised as one of the people were false. Her parents had her true memories replaced with the false ones in a desperate move to protect their only daughter. She would in this way live among the people, think like the people, and behave like the people. Thus anyone searching for a Feyra would only see one of the people. Her parents had been wrong.

The Feyra called themselves The Hidden Ones as they had learned over those same millions of years of development that interacting with the people was almost always not a good thing to do.

But that had changed, in her case, a little. Dee, whose True Name in its most formal form was Daliera Fontala a'Anathor a'Mdator a'Zgura a'Winfa a'Relda d'Dathar Na, although Daliera Fontala was used on most occasions among the Feyra, still published now and then as D. Grant and interacted with a few, a very few selected members of the people.

She took a small sip and tickled the thick fur with her bare toes and nodded to herself. So far that interaction had worked out. But she was very careful and very cautious in what she did with those very few selected ones. Most of the time.

Michigan.

Two weeks had passed and now Ralph and his wife, Sandra, stood on either side of a slim young woman who had just graduated from high school and watched the two coffins sink from sight. The young woman's parent's light airplane had crashed just short of the runway on its landing approach. The parents were Sandra's older sister and Ralph's younger brother.

Today was a sunny day with the clear blue sky dotted

here and there with a few puffy white clouds. On all sides of where they stood stretched carefully maintained and groomed grass with artfully trimmed shrubbery placed just so to please the eyes of the living.

It was much too nice a day, thought Ralph, for something like this. It ought to be dark and raining. It ought to be a miserable day for a miserable event.

It was not the sort of thing that he and his wife had planned for their vacation.

The young woman had been named by her mother by modifying her sister's name into Sandrel.

Sandra and Ralph had agreed that they would care for Sandrel if there ever was such a need. And now that need had risen. In the worst possible way.

Tomorrow, the three of them would drive back to Maryland. A small van would follow with all those things that Sandrel had wanted to keep from her home. Sandra's staff would take care of anything else that required doing.

House Ranadan.

He stood in front of the door and knocked, a very gentle and very polite rapping on the heavy door constructed from wood of a soft red color.

Then he stepped back and waited. It was also a very polite thing to do. House Ranadan was one of the great houses, one of the few so considered to be such by The Feyra.

The door swung inward of silent hinges. A tall male stood in the opening and looked out to see who had come knocking on their door. "Ummmmm."

"Here is Kanatar, come to visit."

The man stepped back and beckoned. "Do come in, Kanatar. Here is Aradon, First Son." Formal greetings were most often given to strangers. "This way."

Kanatar followed him down a long hall, around the next two corners, and into a comfortable room having four chairs and small tables.

The tall female standing here nodded at Kanatar and handed him a filled cup of coffee and one to Aradon. Then she sat in one the chairs and took a sip from the filled cup she held.

Kanatar sat in the chair that faced her. Aradon sat off to one side and watched.

After the proper amount of time had passed, she took another sip, and said, "Here is Anadaz, House Head. Of what do you wish to, ummmm, visit, ah, about?"

Kanatar took a sip. "Here is Kanatar, Second Son of House Mataraen. It was felt by House Head Zarten that it would be, ah, nice, to speak of some bother we do feel."

"Bother?" She took a sip.

"Just so." He took another sip.

"From whence does come this, ah ummmm, bother to your house?"

Kanatar leaned forward and told her in a very soft gentle tone of voice.

Anadaz took a sip. "How does this powerful house cause bother to a great house such as Mataraen?"

Kanatar took a sip, then cleared his throat. "Word has come of the destruction of House Narkalar some not too long ago."

"Just so." She took a sip. "Not undeserved. That house was deeply engaged in very not nice. She had just cause. They did kill her parents and threaten her."

"Ummmmm," he said.

"Did she not see that Eltrill became House Head and

did she not see to their rebuilding, greatly paid for by House Hamptus, who was also greatly involved but still survives? Thus, House Narkalar was not destroyed."

"Just so." Kanatar took a sip. Word had not come to them of that.

"Ummmmmmmm."

Kanatar leaned back. "The Feyra prefer to not allow the people to know of their existence."

She nodded. "For great and ancient reasons."

He took a sip and nodded.

"Although," she said gently, "it has happened a few times in the long ago."

Kanatar nodded and took a sip. "Word has come that the house of which I speak has one of the people visiting at times."

Anadaz stared at him. "One of the people? Visiting?"

He nodded again. "Word has come."

"Ummmmmmm."

"Such strange is bothering."

She leaned toward him. "Have you visited and spoken of this bother?"

Kanatar jerked. "That house is greatly staffed."

"Ummmmmmm."

He leaned forward and spoke softly.

Anadaz nodded. "Word has come of that. Ummmmmmmmm."

"What?"

"Perhaps I would go with you to speak with that house of these, ah, bothers, if you would allow some company."

Kanatar nodded. "One would not like to have their house be no more."

"Ummmmmm." Anadaz took a sip and wondered why House Mataraen was so cautious. She felt that there was more here than it would appear. This would bear some deep thought.

The Big City. The Main Office.

Dee and Janice sat in the guest chairs and waited for the usual storm of grumbling and mumbling to blow itself out as it always did.

Dee had handed him her latest novel and explained why she felt this one had to be handled the way that she wished.

He stared at her as she did, convinced that authors were an unusual breed of life, if not a merely peculiar, but a necessary part of life, especially his life. Finally, he nodded, winced a smile into place, and agreed to whatever they, Dee and her assistant, wished, and watched the two smiling characters leave his office.

As they stood and waited for the elevator to arrive, Janice looked at Dee.

"What do you think we ought to do?"

Dee smiled. "Have a good meal."

"Then?"

"We will just have a very good meal, go visit, and then go home."

A soft ping announced the arrival of the elevator.

Maryland.

It was still vacation time. Of a sort.

Ralph and Sandra were sitting in the kitchen sipping coffee. Breakfast was over, Sandra had made waffles, and now they were by themselves. Sandrel was off to find a dog, something that she had spent some time researching after Ralph had agreed to her request to have one. Sandra had suggested that it was a good idea. So Ralph had agreed. He always paid close attention to anything that his wife suggested.

Ralph stirred his coffee, just a bit, and watched the milk white swirl in the dark black, a very nice spiral.

"This is a real complication," he stated.

"I know, Dear." She smiled at him as he watched his coffee.

"Does she have any idea?" He looked up.

"Not too much of one. My sister didn't think that her daughter needed to know too much about what her Uncle and her Aunt did for a living until she was older."

He reached over and patted her hand. "Charles and Prentice are doing all right with their daughter, Richlin."

She nodded.

He smiled at her. "It will work out. It will be fine."

Someone rapped on their kitchen door.

He stood, walked over, and opened it. And smiled. "Do come in. Both." And stepped back as their visitors walked in.

They sat at the table and waited while Sandra poured two cups of coffee and handed them out. Ralph sat, took a sip, and waited.

The front door banged open and slammed shut. She walked in holding a solid black puppy, wearing a bright red collar, cradled in her arms, stopped, and stared.

"Sandrel," said Sandra, "this is Dee Grant and her assistant, Janice."

Dee nodded. "Pleased to meet you."

"Hi," said Janice. "We just came to visit."

"We were in the big city," added Dee. "On business."

Sandrel sat next to Sandra, scratched a fuzzy ear, and stared at Dee.

Sandra nudged her.

"Oh! Sorry."

"Ummmmm." Dee took a sip from her cup.

Sandrel watched Dee's face. "You the author? That D. Grant?"

"Just so."

Sandrel smiled at her. "I liked the last two books best."

"Oh?"

Sandrel nodded. "Yes. The characters seemed like they were real, much less like fictional characters."

Ralph took a swallow, and looked at his wife.

Dee nodded. "I suppose." And smiled. "No one has said that before."

Sandra stood and beckoned Dee to follow her out into the back yard.

Tall shrubs grew along all the high fences that blocked any view that the neighbors might have of the back yard. In front of the shrubs ran the flower beds, a riot of color, it being that time of year. Sharing the beds with the flowers and the shrubs were all manner of sensing devices. The open interior of the back yard was thick grass having a few benches carefully placed here and there. They were set so that one might sit and talk and admire the display of flowers and, at the right of year, the flowering shrubs.

In the kitchen, Ralph talked with Sandrel about her choice of dog knowing that Sandra would explain the young girl and the dog. Janice sat with them and sipped from her cup and listened. Dee will tell her later about her conversation with Sandra.

Outside, the pair sat on a garden bench as Sandra talked with Dee and explained that Sandrel was her sister's only child. She and her sister had been close since childhood with Sandra visiting as often as she could, which many times, due to the press of what she did for a living often caused a long passage of time between visits, sometimes years. She and Ralph had agreed that they would take care of Sandrel if ever there was such a need. And now there was such a need. A very unexpected need. Her sister had married Ralph's younger brother and at the wedding Sandra had met Ralph. Ralph's brother, Johnston, had taught biology at a high school in Michigan. But the two brothers rarely visited each other. Johnston was smart in a very average way. But Ralph was a true genius, one of those very rare individuals whose intellectual capabilities outstripped almost everyone. For unknown reasons, Johnston had refused to acknowledge that.

From ninth grade on, Charles had been Ralph's best friend, one of a few friends. Charles had grown into a large person. He had always been a rough and ready companion who loved football, watching it or playing it, and all the smashing into one another that went with the game. For some reason having to do with their personalities, the two became and are still deep friends, the one ready for physical action and the other who saw and understood everything.

After college, the pair had done various things together which they explained only as "adventures" and then had ended up in different agencies of the government but continued to meet and talk and discuss and argue which eventually led Ralph to create the idea of The Council. He convinced the President of the time to allow it to come into being as it currently is.

Sandra looked at Dee. "So now I have a grown up

daughter." She laughed. "And a dog!" Then she sighed, a long, drawn out exhalation of breath. "This is going to be difficult, given who we are, what we do, and what we have become."

She stood. "Let's go inside and have some vanilla ice cream."

Inside, dessert was dished up.

Sandrel had some of the vanilla and said to Sandra. "I thought that chocolate was your favorite?"

Sandra nodded. "Tastes change."

Ralph smiled. At his chocolate ice cream.

Sandrel wondered why he did that.

Michigan.

Once upon a time, some number of years ago, the realization came to him.

Stanton Handersal was doing important research in this large library in this large city. It was taking a long time, this research, but finally he had found a key writing that was ancient but true.

Sooooo, he thought, this explains so much of what he felt, of what he had intuitively understood. He almost laughed out loud, but this was a library after all, so he didn't.

He went back to his research now that he saw and understood the path that he was to follow and found a conformation here and another there. "So much to know," he grumbled quietly to himself. "So much has been forgotten."

Then, as he was skimming a history of Europe, he had the revelation and knew what was to be done. At least the first step of what was to be done.

Satisfied with his many long hours of labor he wandered down the street and entered a nearby art gallery just to look at what was offered and to allow his mind to relax. The gallery was filled with carved works of art. He was told, in very low and hushed tones, by the owner that several of the folk in the gallery dressed all in dark clothes were the artisans and that like many an artist were rather reclusive and withdrawn.

He nodded and left and knew, very clearly, what his true path now was.

He had known from a very young age that he was destined to do a great thing. Now, it had finally become clear what that great thing was.

Maine.

The log cabin was at the end of a very long and a very twisting and a very narrow dirt road. A rather dirty, crew cab pickup truck was parked near the building.

The cabin was modest in appearance and had been there a very long time. And over that very long time the different owners had made changes and additions as the mood struck them which resulted in a rather haphazard arrangement.

The end result was that the cabin sprawled in various directions, a bedroom here and a bedroom there. But in spite of this, or perhaps because of this, it was a friendly feeling place.

The well worn furniture was comfortable rather than decorative. Depending upon which room you were in the walls seemed to have a slight tilt in a different direction than the other rooms.

The roof was tight as were the outside doors and windows with nary a leak of water in the summer or snow in the winter. The outside wood of this structure and the color of the metal roof made the structure blend into its setting.

Sandrel and Ralph sat on the edge of the porch, legs dangling, and watched Sandra cooking burgers on a very ugly and ancient grill. The grill had also been there a very long time.

"Couple of minutes," she said back over her shoulder, flipping things over. "Bring out the potato salad. Please."

Sandrel jumped up and hurried inside and returned with a large bowl, set it on the outside table, and rejoined Ralph.

"It is really nice up here," she said.

He nodded.

"And quiet."

He nodded, again.

The puppy wobbled round bellied from the cabin and sat next to her and got one ear scratched.

"I fed her."

Ralph smiled. "Settle on a name yet?"

"Shadowfog."

The puppy sat straighter and stared down the road.

"Someone's coming," observed Ralph.

"Probably Charles," laughed Sandra.

Then they could clearly hear it and see it, surrounded by a cloud of dust. A very large pickup coming their way.

"It is," said Ralph.

Sandrel stood. "I'll get another table serving."

The truck banged to a halt at the far end of the cabin, dust cloud passing into the thick forest. The door flew open and Charles jumped out. "Oh boy! Hamburgers." He laughed, a very happy loud sound.

Sandrel walked back out and handed him utensils and a plate.

He grinned and gave her a hug. "Thanks, kiddo."

"Eat up," commanded Sandra.

They did.

They ate hamburgers, potato salad, chips by the handful, dill pickles, and all the other necessary ingredients that went along with truly enjoying hamburgers.

After they had cleaned up the mess, such as it was, Sandrel hooked a long lead, bright red, to Shadowfog's collar and headed them down a game trail that passed close to the cabin, promising that she wouldn't go far.

Ralph, Sandra, and Charles pulled chairs on the porch close together and sat down, favorite beverage in hand, to talk.

"O.K., Charles," said Ralph. "Spill it."

Charles nodded. "Two of my guys visited the hanger where the crash investigators are working. You know how that goes. Well, after some discussion of this and that . . . ahhhh, crap, Ralph, it wasn't an accident. That airplane was rigged to crash. They are just not sure, yet, how, but that is the consensus of opinion."

Sandra leaned forward and stared at him. "Rigged?"

"Uh huh. Somebody wanted them dead. That means that there are now all manner of folks investigating that event." He sighed. "So, you are you, and he was your brother. Makes things a wee bit complicated."

"Ah well, " said Ralph.

Charles emptied his glass and refilled it from a handy can. "Randy turned a couple of his people loose, checking whatever they might feel like checking."

"Ah." Ralph looked at his wife.

She nodded. "I'll tell her."

Charles lurched to his feet. "Got to go." He handed

Ralph a cell phone. "Throw away, just in case." And headed for his truck.

Ralph and Sandra watched the big truck disappear down the road and the cloud of dust slowly settle.

"Wonder what is going on this time."

"Soon, Dear, soon."

He headed into the cabin to set the phone on the kitchen counter.

Maryland.

Time had passed, four more weeks of vacation had come and gone. It was a rare happening to have that many weeks of peace and quiet, not counting the previous disaster.

The three of them were in the kitchen, two sitting at the kitchen table, one finishing the breakfast preparations.

Ralph and Sandrel were the ones sitting, watching. Sandra gave the eggs a last stir. She broached no interference in her cooking and declined all offers to help.

He banged into the house through the front door, walked into the kitchen, and peered over her shoulder. And laughed.

"Looks pretty good."

She gave him a gentle jab in the stomach with her elbow. "Grab a plate, Charles, and sit down."

He did, taking a knife and fork from the appropriate drawer first. And winked. "So, how you doing, kiddo?"

"Fine," replied Sandrel.

Ralph smiled as Sandra served them all and sat. Sandra looked at Sandrel. "You will learn that Charles has an instinct of a very strange sort. He always turns up when food is about ready to serve."

Charles laughed and spread strawberry jam over his

toast. "Prentice had to go in early."

And then, finally, after the table was mostly cleared, Charles looked from face to face. "I have news."

"Oh?" Ralph held out his coffee cup. Sandra filled it.

Charles nodded. "Randy's guys say that there is absolutely nothing in the background of Sandrel's parents, nothing at all, that would explain why."

"And," prompted Ralph.

"You know how suspicious Randy is and how his mind works."

"And?"

"Well . . . he thinks that it is you and Sandra."

"What?" Ralph stared at his friend. "Do you mean?"

Charles took another piece of toast and slathered more strawberry jam thickly across it. "You looked a lot like your brother and Sandra looked a lot like her sister. So." He took a big bite of toast and chewed. "Randy thinks that you are both dead." And swallowed.

"Oh, my," said Ralph.

Sandra threw her arms around Sandrel. "Oh no!"

Charles nodded. "Someone killed both of you. Except that you are well hidden, as we all are, so to speak. Randy, in his usual worrying way, suggests that whoever it was that did the deed thought that you were using the role of biology teacher as a cover, a very deep cover." He stuffed the remains of the toast into his mouth and chewed. "You know how careful we are, but you are the visible one. Randy's troops are studying every piece of evidence as part of the investigation team, searching for anything that we can follow up."

Ralph looked at Sandra and Sandrel. And blinked.

"We will be fine, Dear. We just need some private

time. I will explain. A little."

"Let's take a ride." Charles stood and headed for the front door.

"Go, Dear."

House Darthar Na.

Janice knocked on the door and walked in.

Dee looked up from her writing. "Ummmmmm."

"I am going to be gone for some."

"Ummmmmm."

"To the Wild Garden. My father just bought a truckload, that is what he said, a truckload of books and other materials from a collector that he knows who is retiring from the collecting game. He told my father that his children wouldn't know what to do with it so he asked my father to buy it."

Dee smiled. She knew that House Hinterane, a house cloaked in deep shadow, Janice's house, lived on the large grounds of what they called The Wild Garden. House Hinterane specialized in collecting all types of ancient materials dealing with the people mythology and folk tales. The House Head was well-known among the people who collect as an elderly gentleman with a vast knowledge of and access to those materials that people who collected such materials, often the very rare, wished to acquire.

"He needs help sorting and cataloging all that stuff. It is going to be a big job."

Dee nodded. "As long as you are in the area, go visit my publisher. Tell him that I am working on another novel. It will make him happy."

Janice nodded. "Back whenever we are done." She walked from the room and down the hall.

Maine.

He sat.

On the front porch of the small log cabin that sprawled at the end of a very long, a very narrow, and a very twisting dirt road. He was watching his adopted daughter play with her jet black puppy, one of the all black German Shepards. He was also watching his wife assemble lunch by the outside grill assisted by his best friend's daughter, Richlin.

Charles had sent her out with them to spend the next several days talking with Sandrel about her new parents, about Charles and Prentice, and all of their occupations and what that meant in terms of what was told to other people, and what was not, including neighbors, very close friends, or anyone asking questions no matter how innocent sounding they might be.

Richlin told Sandrel during one of their many walks along the game trail how it felt to be held captive, twice, once while she was camping with a good friend, how she was freed, and why events like that were only talked about inside the family.

Sandrel often frowned at her when Richlin said that she couldn't answer that question, one of the many that had gotten the same reply. But yes, it all had to do with her parents, and what Ralph and Sandra, and, Randy and Arabelle did for a living. And, oh yes, it was certainly different that what her dead parents had done in their lives. But that she, Richlin, was very proud of her parents and their friends in more ways than she could ever explain.

Lunch was ready. Sandra called to the girls as they strolled from the forest to come and get it.

Ralph laughed and pointed down the road. "Right on time."

Richlin went inside and brought out another plate, knife, fork, and napkin.

The large truck parked at the other end of the cabin. Dust eddied into the forest. Charles piled out, grinning widely. "Oh boy! Lunch!"

As he walked up, Richlin smiled and handed him everything. "Here, Dad." And gave him a big hug.

Then they all served themselves and sat on the porch eating and talking.

Finally, Ralph made shooing motions with his hands and waited until two daughters and one puppy wandered off.

"O.K.," said Charles. "Here's what we know. So far. And it isn't going to be easy to learn more."

"Oh?" Ralph looked at him.

"Yah. It has taken Randy's guys four weeks but we have a pretty good idea for starters. At least we think it is, perhaps, maybe.""

"Starters?" Sandra frowned at him. "Perhaps? Maybe?"

"Uh huh. Remember that company, ah, two, three years back or so with offices and other activities in several countries including our own? The ones where we helped a bunch of white-collar types go to jail?"

"And?" prompted Ralph. Charles liked it, being prompted.

"Randy's guys have identified three powerful politicians and two megabucks corporations whose fingers have recently tangled together and now are involved in seeing to the operation of the reincarnation of that group we jailed. At the moment I am trying to turn that string into a rope." He emptied his glass and refilled it from a handy can by his side. "Enough of that rope and we can hang them. It isn't going to be easy. The first time was hard enough."

Ralph stared down the road. "Not going to be easy is correct. Those types are very good at covering their backsides."

Charles nodded. "Randy and I both feel that pretty soon we ought to know who did the dirty work. Although the group that I mentioned doesn't appear to be involved. Perhaps." He laughed.

Ralph refilled his glass and took a sip. "See any problem that we ought to be concerned with?" He indicated two daughters and one puppy.

"Nope. But they are going to have folk, our folk, always close by." He looked at Sandra. "Richlin thought that having a pet cat around would be good, a very large pet cat." He grinned. "Would you go ask?"

"Now?"

"No rush."

Sandra nodded. "O.K. Can't hurt to ask. You better tell me, us, all the details."

Charles slouched in his chair. And did. It took some time.

Sweden.

The structure, all moss covered stone, bay windows, and towers, stood at the edge of a cliff looking down at the ocean.

She walked inside and was greeted by a short and rather wide woman dressed in bright red clothes.

"Welcome, may I aid in your research?"

She bowed and told her the name that she wished to research.

"Ahhhhhh, that one."

She nodded. "Just so."

"Family atlas files are up this way, all the maps are up a few."

The woman in red started up the broad staircase, saying over her shoulder, "I am sure that we can find what you need."

Her arms were coated with dust up to her elbows from shuffling maps and sheets of writing from pile to pile. She had written copious notes in a small volume she carried in a large patch pocket on her trousers.

Finally done, she stretched and stretched and stretched.

It was time to go. She had one more place still to visit.

House Darthar Na.

Dee, Head of House Darthar Na, looked up from the book that she had been reading as Sandra walked into the room. Dee had been taking a break from writing.

It was one of the small comfortable rooms with a large outside window from which one could look out at the surrounding forest and the great open meadow at the base of the entry stairs.

Sandra was the only one of the people that could do that, travel between places. It was a house skill of House Darthar that Dee had asked her to have, if she could master the skill during a rather long and hard training period. Jonathon, Head of House Darthar, had doubted that one of the people could learn such things.

But Ar of House Darthar Na and Dura of House Darthar, both the guardian, trainer, and repository of that kind of knowledge for their respective houses, had agreed to try. And much to everyone's surprise, including Sandra's, they had succeeded. Sandra's learned skill was limited as she could only do it a few times before she required a great deal of rest before she would be able to once again be capable of that activity. Jonathon felt this limitation was because she was one of the people. Their biology was different.

Dee filled a coffee cup and handed it to Sandra. Then refilled her own. It was proper manners to always give a visitor a filled cup and wait awhile before discussing anything. So Dee sipped, and waited. It was the polite thing to do.

Sandra took a sip, and waited, and then smiled at Dee. "We have a rather strange problem and a request from Richlin."

Dee nodded and took a sip.

When Sandra finished explaining everything, Dee set her cup on one of the small tables, and stood. "Let's go visit Richlin. She is at home, right?"

"Yes." Sandra set her cup next to Dee's and stood.

Maryland.

They were just finishing dinner when someone knocked on their front door.

Charles stood. "I'll get it."

He strolled down the short hall and opened the front door.

"Hi," said Sandra.

Charles smiled at them and stepped back. "Do come in. All." He had learned, from Ralph, that this was the proper thing to say to any of The Feyra waiting to enter a home. They couldn't, they were unable to, enter any Feyra dwelling without being asked to *do come in* and wouldn't enter any non-Feyra house either without being asked, most of the time. It was considered a breach of good manners to enter without being asked. He didn't know that no one, Feyra or one of the people, would be able to enter any Feyra house without be asked to enter by a family member. It was an aspect of the house structure itself. The Flaming Swords, the staff that The Fontala carried, could overwhelm that with ease.

Sandra, Dee, and Purr Cat, the Furleen, a great feline, lion-sized, cougar-looking, all bronze fur with white tiger stripes on her shoulders and neck, walked in. Dee had named this Furleen, Purr Cat, when she was first getting used to the idea that she was one of The Feyra, and The Head of House Darthar Na, and was meeting all the house beasts, a unique aspect of House Darthar Na. A few of the Feyra Houses might have one. House Darthar Na had many.

Prentice, Charles' wife, and Richlin, their college-age daughter smiled at them. Sandrel stared. She was visiting with Richlin. She stared especially hard at the Furleen.

Purr Cat walked around the table and bumped Richlin with her head.

"Heya." Richlin scratched behind one fuzzy ear. She had met the Furleen before.

Dee and Sandra sat at the table and smiled at everyone.

Charles poured a cup of coffee for Dee and handed Sandra a glass of red wine. "We were just going to have dessert. Join us? We have plenty."

Dee sipped and nodded.

"Sure," said Sandra.

Prentice stood. "I'll bring it in." She hurried to the kitchen and wondered what was going on. She knew that The

Feyra called themselves The Hidden Ones and wished to remain so. Yet Dee and the Furleen had just strolled into their house as if they were old friends to everyone here, including Sandrel.

Dessert was a multi-layer vanilla strawberry cake. Charles preferred chocolate ice cream but would eat whatever was served. Dee and Sandra had vanilla ice cream. To The Feyra, chocolate was a horrid taste. Their gift of training had altered Sandra's taste buds. She could no longer stand the taste of chocolate.

Dee nodded to herself. Sandrel was very controlled given the giant feline standing so close to her. It was quite strange for one of the people to be that calm with the unusual.

Charles smiled at Dee. "So, this is a surprise."

"Just so." Dee looked from Charles to Prentice to Richlin. "I would like to change the true promise that each of you gave to me." Before they had done this, she had carefully explained that once given anyone who broke a true promise would die instantly.

"How," asked Prentice.

"If Sandrel will give a true promise to only discuss what she will learn with you three and her parents, I will tell her what she needs to know."

Dee looked at Sandrel and carefully explained how a true promise worked, stressing the fatal nature of breaking that promise.

Sandrel stared at Dee and frowned. "You want me to give you one of these true promises things that I will only discuss whatever I learn with these three and my parents before I know anything?" She finished eating her cake.

"Just so," said Dee.

Sandrel looked at the others.

"We did," said Charles.

"It really is necessary," added Richlin, nodding.

Sandrel frowned and carefully looked from face to face. And then at Dee. "Dee?"

"The people who killed your parents are not nice," stated Dee. "Sandra thinks, and I agree, that you need some additional protection." She carefully watched Sandrel's face. And smiled. "It was Richlin's idea asking for one of The Furleen to come for company and protection." She indicated Purr Cat.

"All right," said Sandrel into the silence of the room. "I will do it." She nodded and looked at the great feline sitting ever so quiet next to Richlin and then at Dee and wondered how Richlin could order something like that around.

Dee smiled at her. "You truly understand what will happen if you break this promise, don't you? Really understand?"

Sandrel nodded.

"You true promise to only talk with the five people I already mentioned?"

"I do."

"You have to say that you give a true promise." Dee looked at her. "I saw what happened, once, when a true promise was broken. That apartment exploded."

"Oh."

"Ummmmm."

"Yes, Dee, I give you my true promise."

Dee nodded.

Sandrel jerked. "OUCH!"

"That was the true promise binding in." Dee stood and

walked around the table to Sandrel and beckoned Sandra over to them. "Let's go to my house."

House Darthar Na.

Sandrel gasped and stared at the long hall of golden oak paneling, glowing soft yellow tones in the sunlight streaming from overhead windows.

"Where are we? How did you do that?"

Dee smiled at her. "Welcome to House Darthar Na, my home. Sandra did it. It was a gift." She led them down the hall and into a small, comfortable room.

After they sat, she said, "Now I will explain." But, as the hostess, before she started the conversation she served them cups of coffee.

Maryland.

Charles looked at his wife and daughter. "Dee always does the unexpected."

"I think that Sandra told her everything that we know about what happened to Sandrel's parents and what Randy thinks." Prentice poured his glass full. Again.

Richlin stroked the thick fur on Purr Cat's neck. "Dee seems to be worried about Sandrel's safety."

Washington, D.C.

Once upon a time, some months ago it happened.

They were gathered in the rather elegant living room of one of the more costly suites in one of the more expensive hotels in the city to talk about various things of mutual interest to them. Mostly about money.

Two Senators, both large and rather overstuffed men, and a Congresswomen, in much better physical shape, sat in large comfortable chairs.

Two wheelers and dealers, one man and one woman, representing their respective corporate interests, sat on the couch facing the others.

The man looked at the elected officials and cleared his throat. "A small matter has come to our attention relative to our mutual interests."

"What?" rumbled Frederick Handewing, known to his electorate as Fat Freddie Hand-To-Hand. It was both a statement as to his physical size and to his ability to see that funding always wandered into the correct hands, from the correct hands.

"We heard," said the man, again clearing his throat, "in the most indirect way possible, that it appears, in spite of all our efforts, that it appears that the mutual interests of the five of us have become known."

"Well," sighed the Congresswoman, "who has shown such an interest. I have heard nothing like that at all." None of her many eyes and ears had picked up anything like that and told her, including those who were located inside the two corporations she was staring at.

The woman on the couch smiled at her. She was one of those eyes and ears. "It came more from a faint rumor than from hard facts." Her smile indicated to the congresswoman that she would have been told had there been better information than that.

The Congresswoman shrugged. After all, this was a city that was always and forever overflowing with rumors of all kinds.

The other corporate representative sat up. He always reminded the Congresswoman of a sleek weasel in human form.

She looked at him. "From where does this rumor come, or who in particular, rather, seems to be interested?"

"We have no idea," said the weasel. "We merely felt that a little heads-up might be in order given the number of committees you three chair or sit on."

Frederick nodded. "O.K. I am sure that we shall pay very close attention to his matter." He sat just a little straighter. "Now, shall we discuss important business matters?"

He reached over and poured a little more into his glass.

House Darthar Na.

"Now you know why I didn't want you to be able to talk about anything that you have learned to anyone else other than those who already know."

Sandrel nodded and gently stroked the neck of the Furleen that sat next to her. She looked from the great cat to Dee and then to Sandra. "Are you magic?" Then back to Dee. "How did Sandra learn to do that, magic?" She thought that it would be fun to learn how to do real magic.

Dee shook her head. "No. We are not magic. Sandra is not magic. It is really hard to explain as none of us really understand how it is that we can do what we can do. Not even Ar, our trainer here for House Darthar Na skills, can. Jonathon thinks that it is some strange genetic mutation that happened millions and millions of years, as the people count time, in the long ago when we split from your line." She refilled their cups. Sandrel looked disappointed.

"You are one of the people, Homo sapiens sapiens. I am, we are, Homo sapiens, ummmm, Feyra, I suppose. We are two sub-species related from that very long ago split into different lines, and are quite different from one another, now. Distant cousins, as it where."

Sandrel ruffled one fuzzy ear. "What is her name?"

Dee shrugged. "I have no idea what they call each other. You could give her a name. She will stay in your home for awhile."

"My home?"

Dee nodded. "Don't frown. No one will be able to see her. The Furleen have a unique skill, somewhat like a chameleon." She nudged the great feline. "Go show her."

The Furleen walked over to the wall and disappeared. Then two great green eyes seemed to peer at them from the wall.

Sandrel laughed and looked at Dee. "I shall call her, Ms. Hyde."

Sandra looked at Dee. "Do you think that is really necessary?"

"Someone killed her parents. They must know that the daughter is still alive even if they don't know where she might be living. Whoever it was that did that are not nice. Sandrel should have protection at all times until we no longer have a concern for her well-being."

Dee looked at Sandrel. "If you feel that you cannot be safe with your new parents for any reason, at any time, I will have you brought here."

"Here?" Sandrel waggled one hand at the room they were in.

"Here. House Darthar Na. We have many rooms. And there are many here to protect you."

"Dee?"

"Ummmmm."

"Why do you care?" Sandrel watched her face very

carefully.

"My parents were killed when I was young, ah, younger, but older than you. By some very not nice ones." Dee refilled their cups and her own. "So I know how that feels." She laughed. "Besides, Ralph and Sandra are new parents and have no idea what being a parent really means. They have serious and important jobs to do, ahhh, at their, umm, jobs."

Sandrel nodded. "O.K., I understand. A little." She stood. "May I go home now?"

Dee nodded. "Do talk with your new parents. They can tell you some of the other things. Maybe my daughters could come and visit?"

Sandrel grinned at her. "I would like that."

Sandra stood, stepped next to Sandrel, and they were gone. Two people and one Furleen.

Maryland.

Ralph smiled at Sandrel. "Guess that Dee was worried."

Sandra scouped the vanilla ice cream and nodded. "Yes. That is why she sent that Furleen to come and stay here for awhile."

Sandrel smiled, a wide happy smile. "I named her Ms. Hyde."

"She will be very good protection." Sandra thumped the filled bowls on the table, spoons poking up from the ice cream.

"Oh?" Ralph took a mouthful. "Pretty good."

"Yes," replied Sandra. "I saw them in action, remember?"

"I didn't."

The Furleen flowed past him and seemed to disappear into the wall near his left side.

"My," said Ralph as two great green eyes appeared to be staring at him from the wall.

"Dee said that you could call them Chameleon Cats because of that," explained Sandrel.

"Ummmmm," said Ralph.

"What?"

"Why aren't you bothered by all this, ah, unusual behavior?" He began to eat his ice cream.

Sandrel shook her head and shrugged. She mashed her ice cream with her spoon. "Dee said that you would explain *not nice* and House Sextet."

Ralph hastily swallowed. "She said that, did she?"

"Yes." Sandrel nodded. "She said that it was a House Head's duty to do that. Oh, and that her daughters might come and visit." She smiled at him. "They may, if you say that it is all right."

So Ralph cleared his throat and began to explain, what he knew. "For the Feyra the term *not nice* is laden with multiple meanings including what you would understand as despicable, sleazy, perverted, dirty rotten mean, and all the other awful things you can think of."

Then he explained that he had agreed that he would become the Head of House Sextet which placed him and Sandra and now Sandrel in a special relationship with Dee as there were mutually intertwined cultural obligations between the two linked houses, one an adopted house, House Sextet, and one a true house, House Darthar Na.

"Really complicated," agreed Sandrel.

"Much more than you can imagine. The Feyra also place very great value," continued Ralph, "on a house having children so that the house is insured of having a future." He smiled at Sandrel and then at Sandra as she dumped more ice cream into his bowl. "Sandrel, you are now, in their cultural view and terminology, The First Daughter of House Sextet."

Then he explained that the First Daughter, or, the First Son, was expected to become the eventual House Head, receiving the title of The Anointed One, if the First Daughter or First Son agreed to be that and take on that obligation.

She frowned, just a little. "Certainly a lot to learn."

"Certainly is. Their culture has some very complicated aspects to it." Ralph smiled. "If Winala comes to visit you can expect her to start telling you all the things you will need to know if you accept the obligation of being The Anointed One."

Michigan.

Once upon a time, some number of years ago, it happened.

Stanton Handersal stood in front of his small but very dedicated congregation in the reworked and rebuilt barn with the carved sign just outside the entry door. The sign told any who wished to walk close enough to read it that this was the home of *The Brothers of The Truth Church.*

"I have had a vision," he told them in a harsh whisper. It had come to him during his library research but he had been waiting a long time before announcing this fact. Now was the time. He was certain of that.

The congregation sighed, a soft sibilant exhale of breath.

"I have had a vision," he intoned. "Henceforth," he pronounced in a soft growl. "Henceforth, we the few, we the very few, we the chosen, are reborn on this day onto a new calling, onto a greater calling, onto a holy mission, onto a great cleansing. I do tell to you this now. THIS! We are The Chosen Few! We are to take to heart the very words of the holy Archbishop John Tillotson, who spoke these words, these ignored words, to us he spoke these words down the flow of time from 1690 to this very day. He said this, he told us this: The greatest heresy in the world is the wicked life!"

"AMEN!" shouted the congregation.

"We are The Ones!" Hendersal leaned toward them, eyes seeming to gleam in the shaft of light he was ever so carefully standing in. "We are The Ones, I say. We are those, in these times of great disbelief, who will obey the Scriptural injunction against witchcraft! Theologians of all creeds believe in the reality of such creatures, of compacts with the devil, and regard those who make those compacts as unfit to live!"

"HOLY, HOLY, HOLY," shouted the congregation as they began to sway from side to side.

He strode back and forth, too filled with energy to stand in one place.

"Henceforth we are reborn, you and I," he whispered to them. "We are reborn, now and forever, into *The Flaming Sword of Truth Church Militant!*" He threw his arms out, palms up, as he gazed upward.

"YAAAAAAA," roared the congregation.

He leaned forward and beckoned them to approach.

"We are the new knights taking up the sword dropped when the Knights Templar were betrayed by that papist politician in that vipers den of Rome who conspired with a money grubbing king of France to destroy them to the very last man."

"OHHHHHHH," moaned the congregation, inching

forward.

"Like those Templars of ancient times we will be clothed in the armor of the true belief, our very souls protected by the armor of our faith. But we cannot be destroyed as were those Knights of old because we bow to no central authority, religious or secular!"

He waved them closer.

"TODAY!" he shouted to the very rafters. "Today," he murmured. " I call on every man, today I call on every woman, today I call on every child, to take up with me the new ways of our new order, to take on the vows of chastity and obedience, to form a disciplined crusader war machine against the evil infecting this very world around us."

He smiled and beckoned to them. "Come forth my children in arms, come forth and join with me. It . . . is . . . our destiny . . . it is . . . our time!"

The congregation surged up and around him, smiling, faces radiant with joy. And thus it came to pass that a new order, a new militant arm of the church was born.

Pondering Change.

House Darthar Na.

Dee was sitting in one of the small comfortable rooms that had a large outside window.

She was sipping coffee and watching morning creep across the forest just beyond the great meadow at the bottom of the entrance stairs.

Jonathon walked into the room. He was using the name Jonathon Harkerness currently because he liked it. His True and Formal Name was Othara a'Anathor a'Mdator a'Zgura a'Winfa a'Relda d'Darthar. And sat. In one of the comfortable chairs. Ar had invited him in. It was unusual, but then, Dee did, and allowed, the unusual.

She stood, fetched a cup, filled it, and handed it to him. Then she topped up her own cup, sat, and waited. And took a sip.

"Ummmmm." He took a sip.

She waited. And took a sip.

"Was that wise?" He took a sip.

So did she. "I hope so. But it felt to me that it was necessary."

"Ummmmm." He took a sip. She did have radical ideas. It must come from her people memories. The Feyra did not interact with the people, almost never. For very good reasons. The people were strange and often did strange. And for the most part seemed to be incapable of understanding, or accepting, non-humans.

"Sandrel spoke to House Head Ralph and he thought that it would be nice if Winala and Tiela came for a visit."

He nodded. And took a sip.

"Sandrel is a very bright young woman. Richlin will visit at the same time. I added Tiela and Winala to their True Promise. Thus, all the daughters will be able to converse freely. And all will learn from each other."

He looked at her. "And all will be safe?"

"Two Furleen and Tiela, who is Fontala who will wear her jacket, her armor, and take her staff, the Flaming Sword."

He nodded.

"There are also certain members that The Council can draw upon who will keep their eyes on all of them as well."

He nodded again.

Maryland.

"Full house," laughed Ralph looking around his dining room table. The table could hold ten people comfortably although it was usually only the six of The Council.

Sandra nodded and refilled his wine glass.

Dessert had been cheesecake. Now every little of it remained.

Shadowfog, Sandrel's puppy, sat on the floor next to Purr Cat who sat next to Richlin. Ralph was amazed. Of course, he had no way of knowing that the Furleen had talked with the puppy and explained what she needed to know. Ms. Hyde sat on the other side of Sandrel.

The four young woman had spent part of the day at a nearby and gigantic shopping mall. Richlin and Sandrel had thought that Tiela and Winala ought to experience this. None of them realized that a number of Charles' people watched them. The Furleen had remained in Sandrel's home.

The two Feyra were startled and rather puzzled by what they saw as the wandered the mall. Neither could understand why the people needed so many things. Tiela had to leave her staff at Sandrel's home. People didn't carry such things around in a mall.

"There are so many of them," mumbled Tiela to her sister.

"It is what I saw when I visited here before."

"How can they live this way?"

"I suspect," suggested Winala, "that they don't know any better. Although I also think that it probably has to do with their breeding behavior." She shrugged. "Of course, it might be because of their very short life spans."

Tiela edged closer to her sister. "There are two males behind us, following us."

"Probably following Richlin and Sandrel."

"Ummmmm."

"Just so."

Ralph looked at them as they finished eating the last of the cheesecake. "So, you guys went to the mall?"

"We did," answered Sandrel.

"It was . . . interesting," added Tiela.

"Buy anything?"

"No," said Richlin.

"No need." Winala took another helping of the meat loaf. This was a new type of food for her. Ralph smiled at her.

After dessert was gone and Winala was finished, Winala and Sandrel went to one of the bedrooms to talk. Sandrel had accepted the title of The Anointed One, the one who would become the next House Head. She felt by doing that it might help Ralph in his relationship with Dee. Tiela and Richlin went to the living room with Ralph and Sandra.

"Is Sandrel really in danger?" Richlin frowned at Ralph.

"We really don't know. Yet. But given what we do know, we are being cautious." Ralph shrugged. "As far as we can tell, no one knows where she is. Her mother, Sandra's sister, never told anyone that we would become her guardians." He smiled at her. "It was one of our organization's attorneys that did all the paperwork so anyone searching in that direction will find nothing at all."

"And no one knows where you, or we, live, do they?"

He nodded at Richlin. "We made a lot of changes about things like that after that last great fiasco. Now, none of our names appear on anything, not on a deed, not on an anything. You are in college so we watch that very closely. Sandrel wants to start college. So we will watch that very closely as well. Of course, your names will be in the college records, only your names and a phone number, an untraceable phone number." He shrugged. "Can't be helped. Names have to be on diplomas and transcripts."

Richlin looked from him to Sandra. "I didn't know that I was being watched carefully."

"That is the way it is supposed to be," stated Sandra. "If necessary, you and Sandrel will be taken to Dee's home. You have had enough of that kind of excitement."

Richlin nodded. She had been rescued twice. Once it was her and her friend. Then it was her, her mother, and Sandra.

"Spring break is over," she said. "Tomorrow it is back to school time for me."

Tiela looked from face to face. "Winala and I will stay for a few more of your days, then we shall return home."

New Mexico.

Far out in the solitude of the empty space of mountains and valleys, with few roads of any kind, they had a place on land that had been bought many years ago. It was a land of greys and browns.

The group lived a quiet life and bothered no-one.

The neighbors, few and far between, thought that it was a retreat of some sort or other, but not one of those "hippy" things left over from the 1960's, for the inhabitants dressed in plain clothes colored a soft brown and were quiet and withdrawn. These folk bought all their supplies in the nearby towns, nearby meaning that it was only a few hours drive, one way, to do that.

The inhabitants were, unknown to their neighbors, members of an ancient order with other small establishments scattered here and there in various parts of the world. This place was now the hub of their organization, the place where they slowly gathered information. It was read and re-read and analyzed and discussed. While this establishment had been utilized for a few generations, the greater group stretched back in time for a number of centuries.

They referred to themselves as "The Searchers," those who sought the truth behind the writings of the solitary soul that had filled the slim volume from which they all took their direction, their purpose, and their ultimate reason for existence.

Boston.

It was Thursday of the first week of classes.

Richlin, her best friend Penny, and their frequent male companion who usually joined them for lunch, sat at one of the many tables.

The group was discussing this and that but nothing that had to do with class work. Their male friend was rattling the ice remains in his orange drink and chewing on one piece of the ice.

Three burley men pushed through one of the many entrances, looked around the large space, and charged over to their table. They shoved Penny one way, their male friend the other, and grabbed Richlin.

Their male friend jumped to his feet, seemed to twitch one arm, and something made three soft pops. The assailants gasped, sagged, and crumpled to the floor, jerked, and lay still.

Screaming, yelling, shouting, and silent students ran in all directions and rapidly cleared a great open space around Richlin's table. Most of the occupants in the large cafeteria hurtled outside. Some huddled on the floor and dialed 911.

"Sam?" Richlin stared at him and the small gun he was holding.

With his free hand, Sam pulled a thin wallet from an inside pocket and flipped it open as he shoved the gun somewhere. And smiled at her.

Richlin stared at it. "You work for my Father?"

Sam ducked his head and replaced the thin wallet in his pocket. "Busted!" He crunched on the ice in his mouth. "Very close surveillance." He shrugged. "Sorry. Doesn't work if you know." He looked at Penny. "Everyone all right? You guys might as well go the class. I'll take care of this mess." He sat in a free chair and grabbed his cup from the table, somehow it had remained standing, slumped, and looked like any other student.

As Richlin and Penny exited by one door a number of

police stormed in through another door, guns pointed in all directions.

Sam watched them head his way and waited for them to calm down.

Michigan.

Once upon a time, some time ago, it happened.

She woke. Again.

And sat up. The chain tightly fastened around her waist clattered metallic chatter. She could walk a short distance in all directions before she was halted by the rather short length of her bindings which were anchored to the rather damp concrete wall of this most unpleasant cellar with no windows. It was hard to know day from night which, she assumed, was the purpose of her captors.

Periodically someone would bring food down the heavy wooden stairs and set the metal tray on the floor just within her reach. They only gave her a spoon and some paper napkins for her to use as most of what she ate was eaten with her fingers.

This time, as she was eating, she heard heavy footsteps thumping down the stairs. It was the ugly one, the male responsible for her being held here.

Stanton Handersal dragged a straight backed wooden chair over, close but not too close, and dropped into it.

"So, witch, ready to do as we wish?" Dark eyes glared at her from beneath an equally dark frown.

"I am not a witch." She wondered if he would ever stop that nonsense.

He waggled a thick book with a very worn cover at her. "Of course you are. We know the truth of that. Witches always lie. Do as we wish and we will return your child to you. We heard that other witch yell to you that your daughter was safe. But, ah, ah, ah, ah, we found her, sssssss, later."

She stared at him and shook her head. "What you want is just not possible. There are no witches and, even if it were possible that there were, I have no way to know or recognize a witch from any other one of the people."

He sighed the sigh of the put upon and thumped the book against one thick thigh.

He smiled. "But we do. You will come with us when we go to inspect one of them. You will do what we wish you to do if you hope to ever see your child again." He nodded. "Young children do need their mothers, almost as much as their mothers need them."

He stood and dragged the chair well beyond her reach. "Eat your food! In one hour we are leaving. It is a nice day. Outside."

He spun and thumped back up the stairs and said to her over his shoulder as he disappeared in the gloom, "We found you, didn't we?"

The Wild Garden. House Hinterane.

It was a large library, all the walls lined with bookcases that rose from the floor to the high ceiling.

She stood in the middle of the floor, all the furnishings, the large table and its chairs shoved over again one bookcase.

All around her there were stacks of books and other printed materials. Some of the stacks only had a few items, some had so many items that it took several stacks to hold them all.

The door opened. She looked up
"Father."
"Third Daughter."

She waved at everything.

"The tall ones contain items that are fairly common, often quite old but fairly common. The smaller stacks are older." She pointed at the smallest. "These are the ones that contain the most ancient and rare of the people books and written materials dealing with their mythology."

He eased his way in and around everything and pulled out one of the chairs and sat.

She smiled at him.

"Now the long process of cataloging and evaluating everything is ready to begin."

He nodded. "It will take a number of people weeks to do that. Do you mind?"

She shook her head. "As the House Head wishes, his daughter will do."

He laughed. "Only if you wish. I have no, ah ummmmm, wish to keep to you separated from Daliera Fontala if there is a need to return."

She wobbled her head from side to side.

"Dee will send word if there is something."

He stood. "Then let us go to a more comfortable room and have something to eat."

She took his arm and walked out of the room and down the hall.

Maryland.

"Your professors all know about the ruckus and know that you will be missing some of your classes for a bit and understand. For you, it is a vacation with Dee. For us, it is a whole bunch of hard work." He hugged his daughter.

Sandra walked into the living room. "A big mess, Charles."

He laughed. "Right about that."

Sandrel followed Sandra into the room and looked at Richlin. "You all right?"

Richlin nodded. "Sam was amazing."

"One of my best," stated her father.

Sandra looked at Richlin, then Sandrel. "Ready?"

Both nodded.

"Back in a bit," said Sandra.

The three were gone.

Charles looked at his wife. "That," he said, "is more amazing than Sam."

Prentice smiled at him. "At least we won't have to worry about the kids, ah, young women."

He laughed and hugged her. "Right!" Releasing her, he walked over to the correct telephone and made a few calls.

Sometime later, the six gathered in Charles' living room, sipping their favorite beverage.

"Learn anything useful from the three stiffs?" asked Charles.

Randy shrugged. "Not much. Thugs for hire, cheap hire. We have teams visiting all known associates and known hangouts. Someone, somewhere, saw or heard something. If it is there, we ought to get it." He nodded at Charles. "Someone made a mistake. They thought that it would be easy. So they hired cheap. Your guy was very good at blending in."

Charles nodded. "He was there from the day she enrolled. He would have graduated when she did although he doesn't need any more degrees. A very special guy." He laughed. "One of the several."

"Something to think about," suggested Ralph.

"What?" Charles refilled his glass and added a few

grains of salt to the thick foam.

"Sandrel disappeared right after her parents died, without a trace. Sandra and I are apparently dead, so to speak, so someone tried for your daughter. Someone, somewhere, somehow, has a vague inkling of our group. It is time to throw a whole bunch of disinformation into the media."

Randy smiled. "I have just the bunch for something like that. Let's meet in a week with ideas of what's next."

"Everybody double up their security," stated Charles. "Those three thugs were in bright daylight in the middle of a campus and thought they could get away with it."

House Darthar Na.

Dee told Richlin and Sandrel that they could wander as they wished although they were restricted to the first two floors. The pair headed down the sun filled hall, talking softly.

Dee smiled. "Thanks, Sandra."

"A pleasure and thank you." She disappeared.

Dee walked down the hall and turned into the correct room. Tiela and Winala were already there, having a snack, accompanied by their Ice Cats, given to them when pets and children were all very young.

Now the Ice Cats, called Hamil by House Darthar sub-House suta Milaton who raised them, were full grown. They looked like sleek polar bears with a head and face that was more cat-like than bear-like. Sitting next to their chosen daughter, the head of the Ice Cat was level with the head of the young woman.

Given their size they did tend to make a small room rather crowded. No one cared about that.

Dee sat and took some of the various items on the table.

She sipped from her cup, then asked, "What do you think, Winala?" And bit into something.

"She is a very fast learner and a very relaxed person."

"I am wondering about that relaxed part. It seems strange to me."

Tiela looked at her. "Mother?"

"Her parents died not too many people weeks ago. She now lives with Ralph and Sandra. She has agreed to be The Anointed One. No questions. No excitement. Makes me wonder. It is strange for one of the people to so behave." Dee took more from the serving bowls.

"Ummmmmm," said Winala, refilling her Mother's cup.

The door to the room banged open and Kitea and Yallan of The Seventh Stand of The Fontala burst in.

"Word," stated Kitea, using the term for the Head of The Fontala.

"Ummmmmm."

"Yallan tells that there is a strange Feyra wandering inside the house! He thought that he had felt something like that for a very brief moment not very long ago."

"You did? A strange Feyra?"

"Just so," stated Yallan.

Dee shook her head. "Not possible. The only way to enter is for someone to ask them to do come in." She turned slightly in her chair. "Kitea, you and Yallan ask as many of The Fontala as you wish to search. Find this strange Feyra. I wish to speak with whoever it is."

"As the Word says, so shall it be," stated Kitea.

Kitea and Yallan hurtled from the room. Closing the

door behind them.

Dee sipped from her cup. "Join us, Ar."

Ar walked into the room and sat.

"If they can't find this one I shall ask the House Beasts to do so. We need to know how this is possible."

Ar nodded.

While they waited, Dee talked with her daughters about various of the lessons and training they were involved in. Ar made a few explanatory remarks.

Then they sat and waited some more.

The door flew open and Kitea and Yallan ushered Sandrel into the room.

Dee looked up.

Yallan stepped closer. "This female is the one!"

Dee bounced to her feet. "WHAT?"

Yallan bowed deeply to Dee. "This is the one. I am The Seeker. It is so."

Dee nodded, his special skill was to know whenever one of The Feyra was around or not too far away. She sent a strong call.

Sandra walked into the room from the hall. "That really hurt, Dee."

Dee bowed to Kitea and Yallan. "Very well done. Go calm the others. Please."

They hurried away.

Dee waved her hand. "SIT!" Dee picked up her cup.

Sandra sat and took a sip from her cup and looked at them.

"Sandra, tell me about your, ummmmm, daughter." Dee settled into her chair, cup in hand.

"About what?" She frowned at Dee.

"When was she born?"

"Oh!" Sandra. "I don't know. No one does. Exactly."

Dee looked at her and waited.

Sandra sighed. "When we were quite young, my sister and I, she had a terrible accident. After a number of surgeries, she was finally healed. But the result was that she would never be able to have children, that is, she could not conceive or bear them."

Dee handed her a refilled cup.

Sandra took a sip. "Her husband understood. My sister became very involved in various organizations all dealing with children. One day she received a strange telephone call from one of the local churches. A baby had been found on their doorstep, something not often done anymore. My sister adopted it, a foundling, and raised her as her own. She knew all the legal things to do and did them."

"We were always told that her daughter inherited her intelligence from her Mother and her approach to life from her Father." Sandra sighed. "It was a comfortable fiction."

She set down her cup. "Why do you want to know that? What has she done?"

"Ummmmmmm. Nothing. Just wanted to know."

"They are behaving, her and Richlin?"

Sandrel frowned at her.

"Just so."

Sandra stood. And was gone, wondering why Dee wanted to know that.

Sandrel frowned at her. "Why did you want to know that?"

"A small curiosity. Daughters, take her upstairs and introduce her to the House Beasts."

Two puzzled daughters and a confused guest, who wondered now what was going on, left the room and walked down the hall to the correct staircase. Sandrel frowned and wondered what sort of thing a House Beast was. Her imagination flashed scenes from any number of the horror moves that she had watched as she started up.

Dee nodded.

Jonathon walked into the room. "Dee?"

She handed him a filled cup. "Why would The Feyra abandon a child?"

He jerked, almost sloshing coffee on the table and her. Almost.

"What?" She stared at him. This was unusual behavior for Jonathon.

"We . . . do . . . not . . . do . . . that!"

Dee sipped and waited.

Jonathon sat and sipped.

Then she told him what she had learned.

He set his cup down and stood. "This will take some research. Hofga will help. I have never heard of such a thing." He was gone.

She sat for some time, taking a sip as she pondered what he had said. Then she sat straight and nodded.

Sandra walked into the room from the hall.

Dee handed her a filled cup.

Sandra sat and took a sip. And then, after the proper time had passed, she asked, "What's going on, Dee?" She was puzzled why she was being yanked in and out, and a little angry as well.

"Did your daughter go to a people school?"

"Not exactly."

"Ummmmmm." Dee took a sip.

"It was something that I didn't know, ah, until recently. Ralph and I were involved in a very complicated thing with us traveling all over the globe for a long time." She took a sip. "When we were going through the house looking for anything that ought to be saved, I found a journal that my sister had kept. I learned about the time when we were out of the country."

Dee took a sip.

"My sister home schooled her daughter until, as she wrote, her daughter reached her adult stature. Then she put her into the local high school. My sister had all the necessary papers, etc., to demonstrate that Sandrel was the right age and was prepared for high school."

Dee took a sip.

"My sister wrote very long passages about how fast her daughter was growing. But she, and her husband, decided not to have her checked by any medical folk as they felt, watching her, that while it was strange, it did not appear abnormal. And when she stopped growing, she appeared to be like any other teenager, so they stopped worrying about it. They decided that it was just some sort of rare thing that had no negative effects. They didn't want their daughter to be looked at as some sort of a freak!"

Sandra leaned back and took a sip. "So?"

Dee took a sip and smiled at her.

"What?

"For Feyra children that is perfectly normal. I watched my children do the very same thing."

"But! But, she is . . . one of the people."

Dee shook her head. "Not so. Yallan is a Seeker. A Seeker has a rare ability to always know when ever another Feyra is around. This ability works over some distance. He felt her presence in my house."

Dee took a sip. "Sandrel is Feyra. But Jonathon says

that The Feyra do not abandon their children. So he and Hofga are starting some sort of research trying to find out how one of our children came to be what you called a foundling."

"I don't believe it."

"And if it is true?"

Sandra frowned at the table top. "Does this mean that she will leave us?"

"No." Dee smiled. "I was raised as one of the people by my parents who were trying to hide me from some very not nice ones. Sandrel should have no problem living among you. We both know and understand the appropriate cultural people behaviors." She nodded. "Beside, Sandrel has accepted the role of Anointed One for House Sextet. So she will continue to live there. It is now a strong obligation."

The door swung open. Winala, Tiela, Sandrel, and one of the Hounds walked into the room. As this was one of the small rooms, it became rather crowded with one very large Hound, two large Ice Cats and all the others.

"Mother?" said Sandrel.

"SIT! ALL!" commanded Dee.

They did, including the Hound.

"This is Moe." She pointed. "They are often called Inferno Hounds," explained Dee. She had named the four Hounds of Darthar Na when she first met them: Manny, Moe, Jack, and Peter.

"This is a dog?" Sandra stared at him. The animal was as big as a small horse and smelled like wood smoke.

"Yes. Of a sort. Tell him to do something."

"Moe," said Sandra. "Stand up."

Moe stared at her.

"Sandrel, same thing. Please."

"Moe! Stand up."

The great beast looked at her and lurched to his feet.

Dee looked at Sandra. "I had Winala and Tiela introduce Sandrel to the House Beasts. You met some of the others, The Furleen. Moe is another species. He obeyed her because she is Feyra and had been introduced to them by a Feyra member of this house. It is hardly ever done."

Sandra jumped up and hugged her daughter who gasped, "Mother?"

"Just a mother to daughter hug, that's all. Happy to have a daughter even if the circumstances are rather strange. And had a horrible beginning."

Dee looked at them and smiled. "Sandrel, you are one of The Feyra, not one of the people. Some friends are trying to find out how this happened."

"Me?"

"It is why you grew so fast into your adult form."

"Oh?"

Sandra released her and sat.

Sandrel looked from Dee to Sandra. "Mother never knew this, did she?"

"No," said Sandra.

Dee shook her head. "She would have no way of knowing that. She was just protecting a daughter with, to her, a strange, ummmm, growth pattern."

"Good to know that I am normal." Sandrel sat. And began to puzzle over that fact and trying to decide what that would be like, being something else. She really didn't feel any different than she always had.

"Perfectly normal for us." Dee nodded. "Now we have two problems to solve. How you came to be abandoned and why your people parents were killed."

"Feyra are researching the first," Dee explained.

Sandra nodded. "Ralph and the others are working on the second."

Searching. Here and There.

Maryland.

The three couples were relaxing in the living room of Ralph and Sandra's house. It was a well proportioned room, suitable for a number of guests. Dinner had been pleasant with good food, as always. Dessert had been great, as always.

Now, each sat in their usual place in the living room sipping their favorite beverage and were ready to discuss business, as always.

"O.K.," said Ralph.

Randy took a delicate sip of very old brandy, savored it, swallowed, and cleared his throat.

"We found a guy who could have fixed that airplane's instruments so that they would land short and hard. Some sort of tricky radio electronics."

"And?"

"Somebody blew his brains out. Which suggests that we found the right guy. Too slowly." He held up a hand. "However, we feel this means that someone is watching the crash investigation, the crash investigators, and anyone else that turns up there. So, they erased their trail."

Charles grumbled loudly. And refilled his glass, and trickled a few grains of salt onto the thick foam.

Randy waggled his hand. "I now have layers of my sneakiest troops watching our investigators who are not making too much of an effort, but enough, to not be seen. They are enclosed in a bubble of watchers three layers deep."

He shrugged. "Shouldn't take too long to spot someone, or someones, I hope."

Anabelle looked at Ralph. "We are building an updated list of groups who have had a violent tendency. It is those that have not just yelled and postured but actually have done something. It shouldn't be all that long of a list."

Prentice nudged Charles.

"Oh!" He took a swallow from his glass. "We are asking everyone that we can find that knew, even a little bit, Sandra's sister and her husband, if they had ever been asked questions about them by strangers. Not much, yet. Just a few trickles that we are tracking outward."

Ralph nodded. "We will meet on these matters in two weeks?"

Randy nodded.

"Sure," said Charles.

Ralph smiled at them. "We are going to be given, I think, a new problem. Ah ah, I don't have any idea, yet. But I was told that if we were that it would be very sensitive. I was told, very strongly, to use kid gloves, a very gentle touch, and to tippy-toe very carefully. And that no one, absolutely no one, should become aware of whatever we decide to do."

Charles laughed, emptied his glass, and refilled it. "Sounds great! When will you find out?"

"No idea. Yet."

Randy stood. "Then it looks like we meet in two weeks." He winked at Sandra. "Good food as always. See you in two."

He headed from the room with Anabelle and was soon followed by Charles and Prentice.

Ralph helped Sandra pick up the glasses and carry things to the kitchen.

House Bontaz.

Hofga stepped up to the door. House Bontaz knew more about The Feyra culture and values that any other house. This included all the subtle nuances

He knocked politely. And waited.

Finally a voice asked, "Yes?"

"Hofga, come to visit."

The door flew open.

"Hofga! So glad to see you again. Do come in!"

Hofga nodded and did.

The speaker led him down a hall and into a room with comfortable chairs. Quickly he filled cups and handed one to Hofga, took the other, and sat. And took a sip.

Hofga took a sip, and smiled. It was very good.

"Ummmmmmm," said Bozna, Head of House Bontaz. It was always pleasant when Hofga came to visit.

"A strange thing has occurred." Hofga took a sip. Then he carefully told Bozna what they had learned about Sandrel. He nodded. "So. It seems strange."

"Oh, just so. Most strange. But!" So, not just a pleasant visit.

"Ummmmmm."

Bozna set his cup on a handy table, sat up, and leaned toward Hofga. "It strikes me as a desperation act!"

"Desperation?"

"Just so. Someone left that child where one of the people would find her and take care of her. Hidden in plain sight, so to speak. I think that whoever did that expected to return and take back their offspring before the people started to become concerned about the not one of the people strangeness of that child."

"Ummmmmmm. So something interfered."

"Just so."

"Ummmmm."

"You did say that this young female is now staying in House Darthar Na."

"Just so."

Bozna nodded. "Word has come that House Darthar Na would be a very safe place to be."

"Just so." Hofga smiled.

"Might this one visit there?"

Hofga shrugged. "Send a call to Daliera Fontala, House Head." He stood. "I will do the same. She is a friend." He emptied his cup and set it on the table. "Good coffee."

"Fontala? Ummmmmm." Bozna walked with him to the entrance door. "Do come again."

Hofga nodded and stepped outside.

Bozna gently closed the door and nodded to himself. It would be interesting to visit House Darthar Na.

A Very Large Place.

It was a large, black stone, gloomy looking castle with pediments and towers all along the upper walls.

Jonathon stepped up to the door and pushed it open. It was a small door built into a very large door. "May I visit?"

"Jonathon," rumbled the large and thick in every direction male looking out at him. "Do come in."

Hongor lumbered off and through a large archway. "This way." And then into a room and dropped into a large chair, one of many that were set around the table. "What?" Then he stood and handed Jonathon a large green mug which he had filled to the brim and thudded back into his seat.

"You have a question on your face, Jonathon."

Jonathon nodded and took a sip. It was quite good.

Hongor was being polite. For once. "Maybe more than one."

Hongor frowned. This didn't sound nice.

"Would you know if any house has disappeared recently?"

"Disappeared?"

"Just so." Jonathon took a sip.

Hongor snorted. "There are a number of hidden houses and a few houses located inside large people clusters. One hardly ever knows whether any of them are still in existence." He stood and lumbered into another room.

Jonathon could hear books thumping onto a table top. And loud grumbling. Then Hongor lumbered back and crashed into his chair. "Nothing."

"Ummmmm." Jonathon took a sip.

"Ummmm."

"Can you tell me which Feyra Houses are located in the people place called Michigan and how to find them?"

Hongor lurched to his feet and lumbered back into the room he had just left. More books thumped on a table top. More loud grumbling echoed from the room.

Finally he clumped back and handed a piece of material to Jonathon. "Two houses, one hidden. Careful cautious, Jonathon. Hidden houses are touchy."

Jonathan set his cup on the table, folded the sheet and put it into a pocket, and stood. "Many thanks."

Hongor walked him to the outside door. "Careful cautious."

Jonathon nodded and stepped outside.

Washington, D.C.

Once upon a time, not too long ago it happened.

F. Fred looked across the large desk at his long-time

staff member. They had started their careers together and had progressed and prospered over these many long years.

Jeramia, his mother had liked the sound of that name but had no idea how to spell it, nodded. His folks had been dirt poor, as it was said where he grew up, and were two of the many that had fallen between the cracks in the educational and economic system of that time and place. He nodded again at F. Fred, as his friend preferred to be called.

"I talked with one of my colleagues and he gave me a name who gave me a name who gave me a name, and so on and so forth."

"Uh huh," said the Congressman.

"I hired some folk to chase that, ummm, rumor that you heard."

"It has been awhile," rumbled F. Fred.

Jeramia nodded and smiled. "I asked for caution not speed."

"Ahhhhh, good thought."

"Those that I, ah, hired gave me a name that they felt was linked to that, ummm, rumor."

"So, who is it, the one linked to this rumor?" F. Fred waggled his glass, swirling the ice around in the dark amber liquid, and took an appreciative swallow.

"Ahhhh, in that name there lies a bit of a problem."

"Sooooo?"

After much throat clearing, Jeramia leaned toward his long-time friend and whispered softly, harshly.

F. Fred took a quick swallow and stared across the desk. "Him?"

"Yes. Ralph Fredrickson."

"You are sure?"

"Yes."

"He talks with the President whenever he wishes to do so."

"Uh huh."

"And runs something no one knows anything about, called The Council, for him."

"Uh huh."

"A group that no one has ever been able to learn anything about."

"Uh huh."

"So?"

Jeramia leaned back and poured a small amount of the same dark amber liquid into his glass.

"You know that his brother and sister-in-law died in an airplane crash? And that some feel that it was really Ralph and his wife in deep cover?"

"Heard something like that."

"It has been rumored to be sabotage and several agencies are buzzing around, some of whom are making rather unhappy noises."

"And?"

"Watch your back and those, ummm, associates of your's. If anything should lead to them being involved, it would be very bad, disastrous even."

F. Fred nodded and refilled his glass.

Jeramia emptied his glass and stood. He hurried from the room.

F. Fred began to chew on the end of a pencil and began to worry, just a little. Most of his pencils had teeth marks.

Florida.

It was a bright sunny day, a few days prior to the conversation between F. Fred and Jeramia.

It was an uninspiring building.

It was an unimposing office.

Both of these things suited the owner and operator of a very specialized business. He and his staff were very well paid to do what they did. But it was just a very good idea to not flaunt their true economic state of being. Customers might get the wrong idea, if any ever chose to visit.

He answered the phone on the first ring. This phone was a bright green, the color of money, at least as it used to be. It was as secure a phone as any phone could be made.

To call him on that phone cost the person on the other end quite a bit, just for the phone call. But then, those who would call could pay for the call.

"Yes?" He waited, pencil in hand, stack of paper sitting there, ready for whatever sort of notes he might take. It was a very thin stack, just a few sheets, destined to go up in a puff of smoke a minute or two after he hung up.

"Ah," he said.

"Ummm."

"I see."

"Are you sure that you want to do this?"

"Sure. Call me in one week."

He hung up, re-read his few notes, picked up the red phone and talked to the best of his best, and explained very carefully what the job was.

"You do realize that if you get caught it could be rather unpleasant?" He laughed. "Just making sure." He nodded to himself. "It will be in your account in a minute or two." He hung up.

Twisting to the side, he pulled up the correct screen on the large display, typed, and watched the money fly, electronically, from one place to another. Then he burned his notes in a special container.

Washington, D.C.

Clicking pictures like many of the other camera handling visitors, she watched her target arrive and casually walk into the building. If what she heard was true, this was a double of some sort. Nodding to her helper, she walked off, just another sight-seer, and strolled along, waiting for the phone call.

Maryland.

Randy took a large bite from his sandwich and nodded at Ralph. They were eating in Randy's organization's cafeteria. "Pretty good."

Ralph did the same and agreed.

Randy set his sandwich on his plate and withdrew a manila envelope from his ever present briefcase and slid it across the table. "They were very careful, very slick, and ought to work for us."

As Ralph slid the photographs from the envelope and spread them out of the table top, Randy tapped one. "She appears to be running this operation." All the pictures had time and date information on them.

Randy pushed two of them together. In each photo the two people were talking on a cell phone, same times, same dates.

Ralph nodded.

Randy pushed other one around. Six people sat around a table eating dinner. "Probably wondering who you were and where you are."

Ralph nodded. "There have got to be more of them somewhere, watching them, looking for watchers."

"Sure," said Randy. "Two guys, two tables over, and one guy and one gal sitting at the bar."

"We could bag the leader of this group, or, the whole bunch."

"Let's see how the next three days go."

"O.K." Ralph stood. "Wonder who they are."

Randy smiled. "Three days. Ah, Ralph?"

Ralph turned back. "Yes."

"Several different groups? Aircraft. Charles. Now you."

"Interesting, isn't it?"

Randy laughed and watched Ralph head for the exit.

New Mexico.

Doma Sparta suddenly gasped, sat up, and stared up at the multitude of stars overhead.

He had been sitting in the pleasantness of night in his chair, a chair that was set in the exact center of the courtyard, pondering over the several bits and pieces that he had read earlier in the evening that had come together in his mind and had suddenly made a kind of sense. At least to him, these few pieces of information had made a kind of sense.

He smiled up at the stars and thought to himself what a wonderful thing a human mind was that it could do things like that. He reached over and turned on a small lamp and quickly wrote in his personal journal those exciting thoughts before he could forget them, much like dreams that made sense then rapidly faded away in the dawn.

Turning off the lamp, he yawned, stood, and stretched. It was time to sleep.

In the clear light of morning he would reread those few bit and pieces and see if his night-time revelations still made sense and were as exciting as he thought they were.

He tucked his journal in a large side pocket and walked to his room.

House Darthar Na.

Dee strode down the hall to the outside door and pulled it open. "Yes?"

"Here is Bozna, come to visit." He smiled warmly at her.

Dee smiled and stepped back. "Do come in, Bozna. Hofga said to expect you."

She led him down the hall and into one of the small comfortable outside rooms with a large window. Filling two cups, she handed him one, sat, and sipped, and waited.

Bozna, sat, sipped, and looked out the window at the forest beyond the large meadow.

"A very pretty setting."

Dee nodded and took a sip.

"Hofga told me of the young female Feyra."

"Her name is Sandrel, raised as one of the people."

"Ummmm." He took a sip.

She watched him.

He nodded. "It was an act of desperation, abandonment, done to save a child."

Dee nodded. "From?"

He took a sip. "Death probably. There must have been an extreme violence there."

"Jonathon and Hofga search." She frowned. "Who could do such? What house could do such not nice without word coming as to why?" She sighed. "Some houses have become no more from doing not nice."

She took a sip and looked into his eyes. "In the very

long ago, it has happened. In the not so long ago it has happened."

"Just so." He took a sip.

"You know, as do all, that I did such, in the not so long ago, removed a house."

He nodded. "Just so. All know of that event." He took a sip. "You had cause. None doubt this."

"Ah ummm."

"But this was different." He took a sip. And shook his head. "I do not know why."

"Ummmmmmmm."

He nodded. "Tell me of The Fontala, The Defenders of The Innocent. Word has come that you are responsible for their reappearance."

She refilled his cup, then her's, and told him how all that had come about, in detail. And about their long sleep.

Washington, D.C.

Randy sat in Charles' office and spread out the photographs.

"Interesting group," said Charles.

"They are very good." Randy smiled. "Had to, ah, borrow some help to punch through all their safeguards."

He slid over another sheet. "They get paid very well."

Charles looked at the numbers and the names. He laughed. "Certainly do."

Randy pushed over a page, his hand covering the image on it. "Guess who paid for them, this time?"

Charles shook his head.

Randy removed his hand. "Surprise."

Charles shook his head. "Fat Freddie ought to know better."

Randy nodded.

"Think that I ought to send someone over there to whisper in his ear?"

Randy shook his head. "Not yet. It doesn't really seem like the sort of thing that he is usually up to. We are, ah, exploring some other corners, wondering why." He smiled. "There is a very interesting guy down in Florida that we want to know much more about."

They were sitting around a small banquet table in a small restaurant in a small room on one of the narrow side streets, finishing a meal, when she cleared her throat just to get their attention.

"I am going to disband the teams. Now! For a while."

All eyes stared at her.

She smiled at them. "It is just a vague feeling, a vague something that bothers." She walked around the table and gathered up all the checks. "My treat. You know the drill. I'll be in touch." And strode from the room.

They scattered, filtering out of the restaurant, one by one, over the next hour or two. They trusted her vague feelings.

Michigan.

Jonathon walked along the side street following the directions that he had been given by Hongor. He felt that it would be best to start with the house that was not hidden. Hongor was correct. When one decided to approach one of the hidden houses one did have to be careful cautious.

So, he walked along, just one of the many others strolling down the street, stopping now and then to peer into windows displaying various wares on sale. He was ever surprised at the amount and variety of things that the people produced and bought and sold. He was one of the many Feyra who looked just like one of the people unless he smiled too broadly. Then his long canines would show. Long canines were most often a male attribute, in some families.

In the very long ago some Feyra male must have been careless in that aspect while visiting one of the people clusters. The result of that broad smile had started the people's vampire mythology, a series of stories that the Feyra wished had never come into existence.

As he stepped up to read a street sign he realized after consulting the small map that he had bought that the house that he sought was just around this corner and in the middle of the block. It would be interesting to visit with them. Not many of The Feyra houses chose to locate themselves right in the middle of such large numbers of the people. Those that did had to be very careful about what their neighbors saw. The long Feyra life span made them obvious to the people over time if the people paid them any attention. Houses like these had to relocate every so often just to avoid that.

Around the corner and down the sidewalk he went.

And stopped.

And stared.

At the rubble.

At the warning signs to keep out.

Now he would have to find a local library to search back issues of the people newspapers to find out what had been reported. Destruction this bad would certainly make news, would certainly have some sort of report in one, or more, of their newspapers.

He nodded to himself. It would appear that Sandrel is a daughter of this house. She is, probably, now The First

Daughter, and perhaps, the only alive daughter of House Kaanatan. So whatever had happened here some member of the House had put her where she had been found.

He stepped as close to the rubble as he could while staying outside the restricted area, eyes scanning the remains for any indication as to what must have occurred and whether any other member could have survived.

Finally, he headed down the street to find the closest library. He would come back later and talk with some of the people who lived in the area.

He didn't notice the eyes watching him, the very careful and curious eyes watching him.

House Darthar Na.

Dee was eating a first meal of the day with Sandrel, Winala, Tiela, and Richlin.

They had been talking about nothing in particular when Dee suddenly up straight. "Oh my!"

All eyes looked at her.

"Mother?" Tiela frowned and glanced at her staff leaning in a corner of the room.

Dee shook her head. "Jonathon has just found out some very not nice thing."

Winala refilled her mother's cup. "Ummmmmm."

Dee took a sip and looked at Sandrel.

"Jonathon has just found a, not too long ago, destroyed Feyra House not too far from where you were placed on the doorstep of one of the people churches. House Kaanatan, one of the few houses that actually are located in and amongst the people, is a pile of rubble. It has not been removed and has become more derelict since the destruction of it. He is going to search back issues of the local newspapers in the local library to see what was reported about that. Then he will talk with the neighbors. That is all that he knows. At the moment."

"Ummmmm." Tiela took a sip.

Winala stared at her sister, frowning darkly.

"Daughter," said Dee to Tiela, "there is nothing for anyone to do. Now. Once Jonathon knows more then we will decide what, or if, there is anything to be done. That house was right in the middle of a great many of the people."

"Dee?" Sandrel stared at her. "What are you talking about?"

Dee took a sip. "Jonathon thinks that you are a survivor of House Kaanatan, that you may be the sole survivor. He thinks that, perhaps, the ones responsible for this can, ummmmm, be identified. Those not nice ones will have to pay for their actions."

"Will you be able to find out?"

Dee shrugged. "Jonathon is very good at research."

"Who is Jonathon?"

Dee smiled at her. "A very good friend. He is also the Head of House Darthar and Lord of the Darthar family, comprised of the Houses Darthar and Darthar Na, and the sub-Houses and my Cousin-Houses."

Sandrel slumped in her chair. "There is so much to learn."

Dee laughed. "I know exactly how you feel. It was all a great surprise to me as well. And sometimes it still is."

She smiled at Sandrel. "Winala is a very good teacher. And I have a guest who would probably help in any way you might wish. He is Bozna, Head of House Bontaz. He knows more about Feyra culture than anyone. When you talk to him ask him to tell you all about two events in our very long ago,

The Great Straightening, and, The Dark Nine Cluster. It will explain much about how we came to be the way we are in cultural terms."

Winala leaned sideways and spoke softly to Sandrel. They left the room.

"Will she be all right?" asked Richlin.

Dee nodded. "I believe that she will."

Washington, D.C.

Congresswoman Sally Anderson sat on the couch quietly talking with her senior staff person, Jons Whitehall.

"You no doubt," said Sally, "have heard the rumor, story, or whatever, about the plane crash that killed Fredrickson and his wife."

Jons smiled. She had a nice smile. It served her well in her position with the Congresswoman. "I have."

Sally nodded. "And you know that his Fatness and J. Robert and I are, umm, engaged with two corporations rebuilding the organization that Fredrickson destroyed by getting all those senior staff put in jail."

Jons nodded. "From what I know, they all deserved it."

"Probably so. However."

"Yes?"

"It does not feel right to me. Plane crash. Corporate rebirth."

Jons nodded. "I will, ah, look into that, all of that." She shrugged. "It shouldn't take long."

Maine.

Janeson Antzonon ran.

His last name was pronounced Ahn-Tzo-non. His first

name was pronounced Jan-eh-son. But somehow he was always winding up with the nickname of Ants.

Ants ran for his life.

He was being chased by some real nut cases. At least that was how he saw them. They probably felt different.

He ran as hard as he had ever run.

Running as hard as he was able to run was something that few other people could do. Jan, as he preferred to be called, was a member of a relatively small number of people who participated in Trail Runs, running along trails in the mountains or in the forest or where ever the trail happened to be. He was one of the few who could run for miles and miles and miles, thirty to fifty miles just being a casual jaunt for him, just for the fun of running.

He was hurtling down the street headed for a trail that he knew began just at the edge of this very small town.

The stars were out, the air was cool, and it was dark inside the forest.

He had run this trail many, many times, and knew every slope and dip, every rock and tree root.

Barely visible in his dark clothes he shot into and down the trail.

His pursuers stopped and stared into the forest black. For the moment, he was out of reach. But they knew his name. He, like everyone else, had signed the registration sheet prior to the lecture, printed actually as that was what the instructions stated.

While the lecture droned on, all the names were checked. They found that he was a free-lance reporter. So it was decided that his career needed to come to an end.

Maryland.

Charles and Prentice were visiting Randy and Anabelle.

It was Saturday and they were having lunch, sitting in the kitchen. The twins were in the back yard playing.

Charles took a large bite from his sandwich, chewed, and looked at Randy.

Randy waggled a dill pickle at him. "So, you agree?"

Charles swallowed. "Yah. Ralph and Sandra go to their cabin and play dead. We pick up these folk and find out what's going on." He nodded and took another sandwich.

Prentice winked at Anabelle and sliced her sandwich from corner to corner.

Randy nodded and took another sandwich. "I will have a few folk monitoring the road to their cabin and any visitors. Nobody will drive up that way unless we wish it."

Charles grinned. "Ralph can use some time for peace and quiet."

He refilled his mug.

Virginia.

Franklyn Haberston, the one that Sally the Congresswoman thought was a sleek weasel in human form, sat behind his desk in his large and well furnished office, in a large and comfortable chair.

His desk sat diagonally across one corner, the corner was formed by glass from ceiling to a low wall stub about three feet high along both walls.

He nodded at the man who sat in an equally large and comfortable chair in front of the desk. Both men held crystal goblets and sipped at the golden liquid that they contained.

The man, who currently called himself James James,

nodded. "Everything says the same thing. Fredrickson and his wife died in a plane crash. It appears that Fredrickson was passing himself off as a professor in a small college. The usual airplane crash investigation goes on. Thus, it appears that the rebuilding of the organization has less to worry about than it did not all that many weeks ago."

Franklyn swirled the liquid around in his goblet, and smiled. "It does appear that way, doesn't it." He silently congratulated himself, took a mouthful, held it, and savored it.

Washington, D.C.

The door opened and interrupted the lobbyist in the midst of his hard sell.

"Madam," said Jons.

Sally stood, and smiled at him. "Do come back, ah, some other time, Henry."

The darkly frowning lobbyist hurried from her office. It was not the usual way he was treated in this town. He was important, after all.

Jons stepped in and carefully closed the door.

Sally sat and waggled one hand at the just vacated chair.

Jons sat and waited.

Oh, oh, thought Sally, this is not a good sign. She waited.

"I just heard this and felt that you needed to know before the media launched into its usual frenzy."

"What?"

"The investigators for that airplane crash . . . "

Sally nodded. She knew which airplane crash was the airplane crash that Jons was talking about.

"The investigators have identified, and are certain, that it was sabotage."

Sally slumped, just a little. "No doubt?"

"None."

"Does put a different light on things, doesn't it?"

"Indeed."

"This being released to the public?"

"Late tonight."

"And it was really Fredrickson?"

Jons shrugged. "It is what the investigators all say, several agencies worth."

Sally nodded. "Cancel all meetings with Freddie and the rest. And do not accept any visits from them either. For some time. Then we shall see."

Jons stood. "Right away."

"And prepare a statement, the usual sort of thing, for the press, terrible news about Fredrickson and all that."

Jons smiled. "Right away."

She closed the door as she left.

Maryland.

Charles was slumped in a couch, sipping his favorite cold beverage from a large mug, and watching a football game.

Prentice walked in and handed him a cell phone. "For you."

He took it, listened, shut it off and took a swallow. And laughed.

She looked at him.

"Wonder how Ralph will enjoy being officially dead. It was just released to the media, sabotage and all that."

He clicked off the game and began switching from

news channel to news channel.

Then he made a call.

Maine.

They were sitting on the front porch of the small cabin enjoying the quiet, each other, and a very good red wine. There was no television out here nor radio. Just lots and lots of quiet.

The phone rang.

Ralph turned it on. "Yes?"

Then he hung up.

"Well," he said.

"Dear?"

He smiled at her. "We are now really and truly dead. Charles said that it is all over the news."

"Then we shall have some quiet time all to ourselves."

He threw an arm around her shoulders as she leaned his way. "Certainly will be different."

The quiet time lasted not all that long.

Interesting, Isn't It?

House Darthar Na.

Dee was strolling along a game trail in the forest. Her companion on this stroll was Purr Cat, a Furleen, one of the House Beasts of House Darthar Na, recently returned from visiting with Richlin.

Dee hadn't done this before, taken a stroll in the forest around her home. But she had decided that it was a nice day and a stroll felt just like the thing to do on such a day.

So, that is what they were doing. Just the two of them, strolling along the game trail, enjoying the day and the exercise.

The forest floor was open with very little undergrowth to block the view. Here and there a bright shaft of sunlight poured through an opening in the thick canopy making a warm spot to walk across.

The pair wandered along and out into another meadow, slightly smaller than the one at the base of the entry stairs to the house.

Here the slope was steeper, much steeper. From the upper edge of the meadow where they stood, they could look out and over the tree tops and across the wide valley at the other side, at the far away forest.

Dee sat on a handy boulder, one of the few, scanned the view, and watched the few high flyers soaring in great lazy circles.

"Looks like fun," she told her companion. Her great feather covered wings appeared and pumped back and forth, a gentle slow waggle of white in the sun. It was a House Darthar Na house skill.

"There are a few people houses in the bottom near the river." Purr Cat bumped Dee's back with her head.

Dee sighed. "You wander all over the place, why can't I take a little fly?"

"You can be seen."

Dee laughed. And stood. The wings disappeared.

"O.K., let's head back." She smiled. No one knew that the Furleen could talk except herself. It had been a surprise the first time that it had happened, the first time that Purr Cat had spoken to her. They only talked to the House Head.

Finally, they crossed the meadow and walked up the entry stairs.

Ar was waiting at the top.

"Jonathon is here," said Ar. "For quite some time."

"I am going to get something to eat. Please ask him to join me."

She walked down the main hall and turned into the correct door, stated her choice, poured two cups of coffee, set them on the small table, sat, and began to put things on her plate from the several serving bowls, and took a sip from her cup.

Jonathon walked in, something rolled into a tight cylinder in one clenched hand, sat, picked up the cup with his free hand, and took a sip.

She ate and waited, and took a sip from her cup.

"Ah ummmm," he said.

"Ummmmm."

Setting his cup down, he unrolled and flattened the crumpled thing, and turned it around so she could read it.

"A people newspaper?"

He tapped a small article with one finger and waited. "Just so."

She finished her meal while she read the article. Then looked up at him.

"This says that Ralph and Sandra are both dead."

"Just so."

She looked at the door.

It opened and Ar walked in. "Princess?"

"Do we have any way to know whether Sandra is alive or dead?"

Ar nodded. "Because I was one of those who trained her, there is a touch between us, a very faint touch because she is one of the people."

"And?" Dee watched his face, a slight blue color. All the house skill trainers had that skin color.

"She is alive."

Dee frowned at the newspaper and then at Jonathon.

"This doesn't make a whole lot of sense."

"Just so." Jonathon took a sip. And waited. The people were always doing strange.

Maine.

They were sitting on the porch of the rather small but sprawling log cabin set right at the edge of the forest at the end of a narrow, twisting, dirt road.

Sandra had made potato salad to go along with the hamburgers.

"All American diet," observed Ralph.

She pushed the large bowl over.

He scooped another helping onto his plate, smiled at her, and took a bite from his second hamburger. He had a large appetite but was one of those persons that didn't seem to gain weight.

Someone hurtled from the game trail that passed close to one end of their cabin, and charged down the center of the road.

They both leapt to their feet.

"HALT!" shouted Ralph. "OR I WILL SHOOT!"

The man skidded to a stop and spun around, mouth dropping open. "Oh!" He stared at them. And at the two guns that were held very steady and pointed at him.

Ralph beckoned with his free hand. "Stand over here, please."

Slowly the man walked toward them, eyes still watching the guns, and stood where indicated. Then he smiled, a cautionary smile. "May I have some water, please?"

"Stay right there," commanded Sandra. "Do not move and I will get you some." She stuffed her weapon into her purse and headed into the house.

"Name," said Ralph. "And what is going on?" He sat, set the gun on the table, and took another bite out of his hamburger.

Sandra walked back from the cabin and set a tall glass and a full pitcher of water on the edge of the porch. "Here." And walked back into the house.

House Darthar Na.

Sandra walked into the room. "Dee?" And nodded to the others. "Jonathon. Ar." She took the offered cup and took a sip.

And after the correct amount of time, she said, "I have

to get right back."

"Take me," said Dee, grabbing the newspaper.

Jonathon nodded. Dee would tell him about what ever was going on this time. The people were always doing such strange.

They were gone.

Sandra and Dee.

Dee felt she shouldn't bother Jonathon to move her from here to there.

Maine.

The man had finished his second glass of water when Dee and Sandra walked from the cabin onto the porch.

"Ralph?" Dee handed him the crumpled newspaper. "What is going on?"

"Visitor." Ralph indicated the sweat stained and somewhat dirty man still holding the glass.

Sandra walked into the cabin and returned, handed Dee a filled cup of coffee. "Loaded the thermos this morning."

Dee took a sip and looked at this stranger. Her gaze shifted to Ralph.

"No idea," said Ralph. "He just, not too long ago, ran from the woods."

"Ummmmm." Dee stared at this person.

"He was quite thirsty," added Sandra.

"Are you hungry?" asked Ralph.

He nodded. "Yes. I am. Very."

Sandra walked in and out, and handed him a plate and utensils. "Dee?"

"Just finished. Most kind."

Dee sat, took a sip, and watched this person step up on

the porch, take a seat, heap his plate, and begin to eat.

"Burned up a whole lot of calories," he mumbled around a mouthful of potato salad. He wondered exactly who were these people way up here at the end of the road with this rustic rather sprawling cabin. And how many guests that they actually had.

Washington, D.C.

J. Robert Brown, Congressman, sat at a table in a far corner of the restaurant, and twirled his fork around in the bowl of his large spoon making a small ball of spaghetti. He never used his first name, John, as he felt that John Brown would make people think of someone else in past political history. He wished that his parents had shown better taste than naming him that.

He chewed, swallowed, and smiled at the young woman sitting across from him as she cut a piece from her lasagna. She was the other corporation, so to speak. This was a private meeting not to be discussed with any of the others.

"What started as a good idea," he said, "now feels to me like something that can be best described as a fall from a precipice." He cleared his throat. "And I am not interested in something like that.

He neatly cut a meatball in half with his fork. "And I believe that you are too smart to do something like that as well."

She took a sip from her glass of white wine and smiled at him. "And so?"

"And so," he replied as he chewed on one half of that meatball. "I am done with that whole project."

"And so?"

"And so, I do not trust Franklyn, not at all." He looked

at her. "If it was me, I would tell whoever you work for to do something else."

She nodded, a nod that signified nothing at all.

They finished their dinner and went their separate ways.

Michigan.

Doma Sparta stood and stared at the rubble of the burned structure. Then he wandered here and there and talked with various of the nearby residents.

All their stories were pretty much the same.

The neighbors in that building, they told him, the one that had burned down, were very quiet and didn't talk with anyone hardly at all. It was very late at night when it all happened. It was the fire bursting through the windows that caught the attention of the few that were still awake. Some tried to enter the building but the heat was already much too intense to do that.

The cause of the blaze was still under investigation for suspected arson. It seemed to have a rather low priority. From what they had heard, no one had survived. It was too bad, really. The people in there had all been artists, highly regarded for their three-dimension art work.

Some pointed down the street indicating where the gallery that handled their work was located.

Doma thanked them and strolled in that direction pondering what he had thought, the thought that had brought him here, and what he had been told. It all felt rather unusual to him. He also wondered who that other investigator was.

Washington, D.C.

Jeramia dropped into the chair and stared at his friend and boss.

"What?" asked F. Fred.

"Sally isn't interested in any meeting with you or the others for some time. J. Robert called and stated very strongly that he was no longer interested in that project, and stressed, very strongly, that you ought to end that endeavor as well."

F. Fred poured some amber liquid into this coffee and looked the question at his senior staff person and close friend.

Jeramia nodded. "I think that it is a good idea. J. Robert jumped ship just before all that news broke loose."

F. Fred took an appreciate swallow of his coffee. "Right!" He sighed, heavily. He knew which news that was.

Jeramia nodded. He knew that F. Fred hated to see all that money get away. But he also knew, in this case, that it was the thing to do.

Maine.

"O.K.," said Ralph. "You have been fed and watered." He smiled. "So tell us your name and why you just ran from those woods."

He nodded, swallowed the last bit of his meal, and licked his lips. "My name is Janeson Antzonon." He carefully pronounced the names. "But do call me Jan."

Then he explained that he was a part-time free-lance journalist. He pointed at the forest. He had been in a small town, told them the name, and had seen an interesting notice on a store bulletin board of what seemed like a peculiar lecture that very evening.

The lecture promised to inform those with open minds, Christian open minds, of the reality of witches living among us. So he decided to attend. He thought that it might make an entertaining article that he could sell.

That small town was not associated with Salem and all their commercialization of their past history. It would be fun to write about whatever that lecture promised. So, he had dinner, paid the entrance fee, printed his name in the log, sat in the back of the small room, and took notes.

Part way through the presentation he came to the conclusion that the speaker was more than a little odd and had a rather extreme overabundance of religious zeal. The speaker had stated firmly, and often, that witches were real and needed to be removed from proper society before they corrupted the youth. He called for members of the audience to join their crusade, a modern crusade. But everyone would have to undergo a careful screening before they could become part of that grand movement. This was to keep the witches from infiltrating and interfering with them.

After the meeting ended, Jan realized that he was being followed by several members of the organizing group. So he ran. And they gave chase.

Then he explained to them about Trail Running and why he felt that he could get away from his pursuers.

"So," he said. "Here I am. In your debt for the food." He laughed. "And the water."

Jan pointed at the game trail. "They might follow that during the daylight and come out here. Once that I knew that I wasn't being followed I just sorta strolled along, in no hurry at all. Then I saw the opening coming and decided to make a run for it in case they were waiting for me here. I had better leave before my trouble spills over onto you." He stood.

"Sit!" said Dee. "Tell me more about these witch haters."

He sat and shrugged. "Pretty much told you all that I know."

"Ummmm." She took a sip.

He looked at this rather slim, small woman, dressed in dark clothes. "I wouldn't go looking for that bunch. I think that they are very dangerous."

Dee took a sip.

"You could get hurt."

"No," said Dee. "I do not think so." She looked at Ralph. Jan stared at her.

"Sure," said Ralph to Dee. "We will look into it." He looked at their visitor. "They probably know who you are if you signed their guest list."

Jan gasped. "Hadn't thought of that." He took another drink of water. "Can't go home then. I live alone, so that is O.K. And friends don't visit because they never know whether I will be there or not. I always let them know when I am at home."

Ralph's cell phone chirped. He listened. "Yes?"

He smiled. "No." And hung up and looked at Sandra. Down the road had just checked in with them. An observer had seen and watched Jan.

She nodded. "We have a small guest bedroom, Jan. It will be quite safe for you to stay here."

He stood. "Thank you. But if they find me here you could be in danger."

Dee looked at Ralph who looked at Jan and said, "Jan, you are staying here." He stood. "Dee and I are going to take a short walk. We have some, ah, business to discuss." He nodded to Sandra as he walked with Dee to the game trail and then into the forest. "I'll tell you all about that newspaper article," he said to Dee as they disappeared into the woods.

Sandra looked across the table at Jan. She took a small leather case from her purse, and flipped it open. And showed it to him. "You are going to be our guest for a while."

Jan stared at the identification and the insignia and sat.

"And," she said, "you may not write a word of any of it, only your adventures with those witch hunters."

He nodded, slowly. "What are you doing way out here?"

She smiled. "Taking a vacation."

Washington, D.C.

Charles sat at a desk in a room that Randy had made available. He took a sip from his cup of coffee, just black coffee, and looked at her, the very pretty woman who sat in one of the guest chairs, looking very relaxed considering where she was and how she had gotten here. He thought that she had a rather exotic appearance. Black hair, light tan skin, high cheek bones, dark brown somewhat oval eyes.

Setting his cup down, he pulled a folder over, opened it, read something, looked at her, and smiled.

"Very impressive. Very talented."

She gave him a small nod of her head.

"If we are going to talk, I really need to know who I am talking to." He held up a sheet of paper. "Let's see. You are Adaha Priest. You are Helene Hathaway. You are Sonia Fortin. You are . . . "

"Ziaza Sowden," she interrupted. "That is who I am, who I truly am."

Charles smiled at her. "Very interesting. That one we didn't find."

She shrugged.

"So, Ms. Sowden."

"Ziaza," she said. "No need to be formal."

He laughed. "I am Charles."

She nodded.

"Well, Ziaza, we know quite a bit about your, ah, well-paid activities, and, ah, where all that money is, at the moment."

She stared at him.

"Your employer has lots of records. And we, ah, know who paid him as well."

She nodded and set her coffee cup on the desk.

"More coffee?"

"No."

"Sooooooo," he said. "You are asked to, ahhhh, gather information but no one tells you how or why or whatever?"

"Correct."

"You do realize, I hope, that spying on Ralph Fredrickson is bound to make certain folk very apprehensive if, or when, they find out you are doing that?"

She nodded. "He is dead. That was a double."

"And that," he continued, "they might lock you up somewhere anyway?"

She nodded.

"And if they decide to do that, then all your funds are liable to disappear, be gone forever?"

She blanched, just a little.

"What do you want?" she rasped. And cleared her throat.

Charles waggled a hand. "All of your, ummm, helpers are down the hall holding conversations with some of my staff, one on one conversations."

Ziaza sat up, frowning darkly at him, wondering if she ran would she get very far. "What do you want . . . Charles?"

He leaned back in his chair. "As far as we can tell, as far as we can determine, you hadn't filed your report yet. Did you?"

"No."

Charles smiled. "Good to hear that." He leaned forward, thick forearms sprawling on the desk top. "We would like you to file your report with a little oversight by us as to its contents. Think that you can do that?"

"Do I have a choice?"

He nodded. "The lessor of several evils, you might say."

She smiled. "I see."

"True?"

She nodded. "I stay out of jail or whatever?"

"True."

"You leave my money alone?"

"True."

"Goes for my crew as well?"

"True."

"And my, ah, employer?"

Charles grinned. "Other than a minor change in how he does business he may continue to do what he did and does." He shook his head. "No. He won't tell you what that is and neither will I."

"O.K., a deal."

He stood, reached out, and shook her hand. And held it. "One other thing."

She looked down at her hand wrapped inside his large one. "Oh, oh."

"Yep. We may call upon your considerable skills now and then. With pay, of course. And your crew isn't to know why or how come."

"Fine."

He released her hand and pushed a button on the desk top. "Someone will take all of you to a very good restaurant of your choice. The bill is on us. Tell them whatever you wish, but not what we talked about in here. Consider it a slight payment for the inconvenience we have caused you."

She nodded.

He laughed, a very happy booming laugh. "And don't call us, we will call you." And dropped into his chair. "Nice talking with you, Ziaza." He leaned back.

The door opened, a young woman stepped in. "Follow me, please."

Ziaza stood, smiled and winked at him, and did.

In a moment a side door opened and Randy walked into the room. "That went well."

Charles nodded. He thought so.

House Darthar Na.

Hofga stomped into the room shortly after Dee had just told Jonathon about Ralph and Sandra pretending to be dead.

"The people really do strange things." Jonathon took a sip from his just refilled by Dee cup of coffee. She handed another to Hofga.

He took it and thumped into a chair. "Ar let me in."

"Always welcome, " she said to him.

"House Kaanatan?" grumbled Hofga.

"Just so," stated Jonathon. He took a sip.

Maine.

Stanton Handersal gathered the selected few for this important mission in his office and smiled at them as they sat in the chairs in front of his desk.

"As you know," he pointed at one of them, "one of us has just returned with important news, good news, mighty news."

They smiled.

"That so-called newspaper man, certainly a witch friend if not a witch in fact, ran quite a long way down that trail in total darkness, a true indicator of his hidden nature. There is at the end of that trail, a large opening and a small cabin tucked into the edge of the forest. The one just returned saw that witch friend talking with some other people. They must be in league with him."

Stanton lurched to his feet, spun, and looked out the large window, and nodded to himself as he studied the small structure below his office window. Then he spun around and dropped back into his chair.

"We," he stated firmly, staring into each pair of eyes watching him. "We," he restated, jabbing a finger at each of them in turn. "We are going to snatch that witch friend and his cohorts. Tonight!"

He nodded. This time to them.

"In the early dusk, get our witch finder from her, ahhhhhh, room, give her a hardy meal, and then prepare yourselves for action. When you get close to that cabin be very careful. It will be dark, the best time for witches. So, hang onto our finder, tie her to a tree if you feel that it is necessary, and grab those witch friends out of their beds. Take plenty of duct tape and lots of rope. Bring the whole lot of them back here."

Stanton smiled. "Here, in our new place, in our very own small land, we will have all the time we will ever need to interrogate them. They will, I repeat, they will tell us who the rest of their coven are and where they live."

He nodded his head, a violent jerking up and down. "Oh yes, they will tell us all that we wish to know. Even if it takes days." One hand waggled loosely. "Here we are alone with no noisy neighbors to hear whatever sounds might escape these walls."

Lurching to his feet, he bowed his head. "You have my blessings. Eat hardy, and remember, we have the right and we have the might to do this thing."

Delaware.

Sally Ann Dutog, know to her colleagues as S.A., sat on the couch in the large office and smiled across the highly polished surface of the desk at her boss. He sat in his special chair. It was slightly elevated as he was rather short.

Henry A. Ansen was Head of Special Projects in this large corporation. He was frowning at her.

"I think that we should take a very careful look at what is actually going on versus what appears to be going on." She smiled at him again. She had just related everything that she had learned relative to the various politicians jumping ship, so to speak.

Henry's frown slowly dissipated. He had found a silver lining in those dark clouds created by the news from S.A. He was already outlining a new approach and mentally drafting the memo about that, one that sounded very good, very solid, and not a money losing disaster.

He actually smiled. A very rare occurrence.

She nodded. Henry was fast, a very quick mind at finding solutions that benefitted the corporation, and himself, and his staff.

He stood, walked around that vast desk, slid out a

drawer on a small table, took out something, came back and handed them to her.

"Here! Two tickets to the ballet, S.A. They are doing Firebird."

Maine.

It was a full moon night with only a soft light filtering down through the canopy of the thick forest.

They were settled in the dense shadows. They were invisible to all but the most nocturnal of creatures in these woods.

Dee had come up to their floor, the living area that she had given them in House Darthar Na, and sat and talked quietly with Moonat, Cluster Head of the Shadow Feyra. They were a very small group that had in the very long ago separated from the rest of the Feyra and had become nocturnal. They labeled all the other Feyra, "Sun Walkers."

So, they sat, did Dee and Moonat, talking quietly. And he had agreed, they would do this thing for Dee.

The selected ones settled into the black of the forest floor, their dark brown almost black clothes and dark skin color faded them into the night environment, an environment where they were most at home.

They waited. They were very good at waiting. And watched the game trail. They were just a part of the forest night world with the rest of its inhabitants. They would do this for many people days.

Michigan.

"Ah, dota!"

"Just so," agreed Jonathon.

They stood, Jonathon and Hofga, and examined the

wreckage of House Kaanatan.

Hofga slipped under the police tape and began to wander here and there, carefully searching.

The neighbor's shrugged as they peered cautiously from behind their curtained windows. Both of the men had talked, very politely, to them all and had explained that they were family of those that had perished. Some had not met the large man before.

The neighbors had shrugged. If they wanted to poke around in that mess then it was their business and no concern of anyone else.

Virginia.

She was with her crew in one of their favorite restaurants. And here they were, enjoying a wide range of items from the dinner menu.

"So," said William. No one ever called him anything else.

Ziaza smiled at him and then at the rest seated around the table. "First, no one gets excited, at least until I finish speaking." Her eyes checked each face and each expression. Then she told them about her conversation with Charles, heavily edited.

She laughed. "And I didn't even find out what agency or what group that he represented although I know where he keeps his offices, if that is what they really are. But whoever they are, they swing a lot of weight, it seems. So, questions, etc.?"

Finally William cleared his throat.

"Yes?" She nodded at him.

"We may keep on doing what we were doing?"

She nodded. "It was legal. It is legal."

"And whoever they are, they will leave us alone?"

She nodded.

"How come?"

She shrugged. "I think that they believe that our services might be required at some time or other."

"Why?"

"Deniability."

"Huh?"

"If anyone learns what we are doing, for them, we cannot be traced back to any agency of government."

"Oh boy!"

He frowned at the table top, then up at her. "They will keep us out of jail?"

She shrugged. "If they should call, I will certainly make that a condition." She smiled at him. "Of course, they already did that, didn't they. And no one is the wiser, as far as I can tell."

Washington, D.C.

The pair were wandering around with all the other visitors in the Library of Congress, talking softly. The great open space absorbed their voices amid all the other visitor conversations.

"And why are we here?" asked F. Fred.

Jeramia had his arm looped around one of the arms of his boss and friend. "Because I found a note right in the center of my desk when I came in this morning. A note that wasn't there when I locked up last evening."

"Ah," said F. Fred. "And?"

Jeramia swallowed hard. "It said that hiring someone to, ah, follow Fredrickson around was not a wise thing to do. It also stated who I had talked to and the amount paid for services rendered."

F. Fred jerked to a halt.

"WHAT!" He hastily lowered his voice as heads swivelled in their direction. "What?" he whispered.

Jeramia handed him a small piece of folded paper. "Found this is my jacket pocket. It wasn't there when we entered the building."

F. Fred opened the piece of paper and stared at it.

On it, written in bold, black letters was one word.

"SHHHHHH!"

Jons ushered her into the Congresswoman's office and closed the door and waited.

Sally finished writing her sentence on the report and looked up.

"This," explained Jons, " is Sally Ann Dutog. She has an, ah, offer to make."

The Congresswoman smiled at her. "So, we are both Sally. Please sit. Coffee?" Jons didn't know all the eyes and ears she had placed around town and elsewhere, just some of them, nor of her previous meeting with Ms. Dutog and the other Congressmen, just with the Congressmen.

"Coffee would be nice," she said. "However, people usually, at work, call me S.A."

Jons left and returned with a carafe and three cups.

Maine.

Ralph, Sandra, and Jan, early risers all, sat in chairs on the porch of the small cabin, steaming coffee cups cradled in their hands, and watched dawn slowly turning into day. And stared.

Strolling from the forest, from the game trail, they

came. They were very large individuals, dressed in loose fitting brown almost black clothing, head scarves loosely wrapped around their heads, shading their eyes.

Three of them carried, quite casually, a body draped over a shoulder. Three others herded along a woman dressed in black that had a thick chain wrapped around her waist, the ends held by two of the others. The third was walking behind her murmuring softly to her. Her eyes jerked and twitched and then stared at the trio sitting on the porch staring at them. The group stopped and stood in the shadow of the forest.

The seventh member strolled silently over to the porch, bowed to Sandra, and straightened up.

"Bring Dee," he said and watched her as she hurried into the cabin.

Jan stared at them and gulped his coffee.

House Darthar Na.

Purr Cat rose and slipped silently to the side of the door in the darkness of Dee's room. She had been sleeping on the floor next to the bed after Dee had grumbled about the giant feline taking up too much of the bed space.

Someone had knocked on the door. Hard.

"Dee! Wake up!"

Grumbling loudly, she lurched up and touched a lamp, flooding the room with golden glow.

"What? Come in!"

Sandra banged into the room.

"What?" she grumbled again. "Why are you?"

"Come with me. Please. It is easier to see than to explain."

Dee stared at her. Sandra was obviously agitated,

which was strange for Sandra.

Dee slipped from her bed, dressed, and looked at The Furleen. "You better come along."

Maine.

Sandra and Dee walked from the cabin, the gigantic cat-like creature behind them.

"What" gasped Jan. "What . . . is . . . that . . . thing?"

"Shhhhh," said Ralph. "Morning, Dee." He filled a cup and held it out to her. "Sorry for the bother." And waved his hand. "But they insisted."

Dee spun and looked into the shadow edge of the forest, then strolled over to them. "Warm greetings," she said.

The seventh bowed to her. He pointed into the woods. "It was as you so stated it would be, but different."

Three stepped forward and dumped the bodies on the dirt of the large parking space along with a large collection of coiled rope and rolls of duct tape. "These are people, not nice people" said the seventh. The three stepped back.

Three others led her forward.

"One of your kind, Sun Walker."

Dee stared at the woman and the chains.

"Did you do this to her?"

He pointed at the bodies. "Them."

Dee stepped closer. "Remove those things. Please."

He stepped over, reached down, and snapped the chain, dropping the pieces on the dirt.

"Who are you," whispered the woman. "I can feel you but not them."

Dee frowned at her, she must have a special skill, then bowed, and straightened up. "I am Daliera Fontala, Head of House Darthar Na." She indicated the others. "They are The

Shadow Feyra and have a special skill to not be felt."

Dee stepped back. "Who are you? And why were you chained like that?"

Dee half-turned, walked over, and beckoned her to the porch, told her to sit in a vacant chair, and handed her a cup of coffee. It was Dee's. She hadn't had time to take a sip.

Sandra hurried in and out of the house and handed Dee another filled cup. Then she looked at the group standing in the shadows. "I can make another pot." She set the nearly empty one she held on the table.

Dee shook her head, took a sip, and waited.

Jonathon stepped from somewhere. "Dee?"

She indicated the seven. "It is time for them to go home."

He bowed. "Just so, Princess." Jonathon walked over to them. And all were gone.

Jan grabbed the coffee pot and hastily filled his cup. This sort of thing can't be happening. Then he stared at the three bodies lying in the dirt. He recognized one of them, and gulped his coffee.

"Shhhh," said Ralph calmly refilling his own cup, watching Dee and this other person. And waited.

Finally the woman began to talk.

It was late at night, she told them, and the house was sound asleep.

Numbers of them burst into the house killing everyone that they saw with people weapons that made little noise. Her sister ran out a back way taking her daughter to safety. And returned shortly to attack these not nice people. She was killed.

Then they dragged this one from the house wrapped in blankets thrown over her.

Later, after the group had relocated, she was chained to a post in a small structure with no windows and only one door. They told her that if she helped them hunt for witches that they would return her child to her. But they wouldn't let her see the child. And it had been some little long and still they dragged her here and there.

She leaped to her feet, spun, and bowed deeply to Dee. "Great debt to be free."

Dee looked sideways. "Take us home, Sandra."

They were gone.

Jan gulped the rest of his coffee and looked at Ralph. "Do you have anything stronger." Other than the three bodies lying there with the clutter of rope and duct tape, they were now alone. People just didn't do that, appear and disappear. Or casually dump dead bodies on the road.

House Darthar Na.

Dee led her down the hall and into one of the rooms. "You are probably hungry," she said to her. "We can eat and talk." Sandra returned to the cabin.

As she served the female and herself, Ar walked into the room. "Princess?"

"Ask Sandrel to come join us, please."

"Of course, Princess." He stepped from the room.

Dee sat and ate and took a sip now and then.

The woman stared at Dee as she chewed on something. "She is one of the people! The one who brought us?"

"Just so," replied Dee. "I will explain later."

The woman nodded. "I am Ternala of House Kaanatan. The last of the house."

"Your sister ran with your daughter and returned without her?"

Ternala nodded. "Now lost forever. Taken by those not nice ones."

Sandrel walked in. "Dee, Ar said you wanted me to come."

Dee nodded and waved at a chair. "Do join us."

Sandrel sat, took the filled cup from Dee, took a sip, and stared at this stranger.

"This is Ternala," said Dee. "Of House Kaanatan. Your mother."

Ternala gasped.

Sandrel stared even harder at her. "My mother?"

"Most true," stated Dee. "Very strange and very not nice is happening out there." She nodded at them.

Jonathon walked in.

"This is Ternala," she said. "Of House Kaanatan, Sandrel's mother. Mother and daughter will stay here. They have much to talk about."

Jonathon nodded. And followed Dee from the room.

Maine.

In his office Stanton Handersal turned from his large window, sat behind his desk, and looked at the two sitting there.

"Gone?"

One nodded. "We followed their foot prints down that trail and into a small clearing, our three and the witch finder. Our boots make an obvious tred mark. Her shoes make little and are hard to recognize." He swallowed loudly.

The other said, "They walked into that small opening but did not walk out. We searched all around that meadow and found no trace of them."

Stanton stared upward and rocked back and forth in

his chair, then thumped back down to lean his arms on the desk top.

"There must be powerful witches close by, perhaps in the nearby towns. We shall have to be ever so much more vigilant."

He waggled a hand at them. "Leave. I must think deep upon this matter."

They hurried from the room as Stanton stood to stare out his window again.

House Ranadan.

She beckoned in her First Son and First Daughter.

As they walked in both stopped and bowed, and said, in unison, "Mother?"

Anadaz motioned them to chairs and handed them cups of coffee, and waited.

Finally she said, "I have a thing that needs doing and which must remain our secret. You will use all your skills to see that this is so."

Aradon, The First Son, nodded. "Of course."

"What?" asked Fratl, First Daughter.

"I was visited by the Second Son of House Mataraen to discuss things that they felt were bothering. I have thought long and hard and wish you to find the information that I must have in order to know whether our house will get involved in this matter brought to us."

"Ummmmmm," said Aradon.

"There is a house which maintains records of all the houses. The Head of that house, Hongor, is, ummmmmm, somewhat different if not strange and, ummmmm, oft times very difficult to deal with. That house has a most ancient lineage and at times shows that very long ago aspect of the

Feyra. Be most polite."

Fratl nodded. "And what do we wish to know."

Anadaz smiled at them. "I want to know the total history of House Mataraen as far back into the very long ago as Hongor has records. So that is your chore. Get that one to make that search."

She smiled at them. "If necessary tell that one that House Ranadan will be in debt for anything he can do."

"True?" asked Aradon.

"Just so," replied his mother.

The pair stood, linked hands, and were gone.

"Now we shall see what we shall see," said Anadaz to herself. And wondered why her Second Daughter was so long on her search.

Maine.

Sandra and Dee stepped from the edge of the forest, walked over and joined Ralph and Jan on the porch.

Sandra went inside and returned with the coffee pot, filled cups and handed them around. Then she sat and waited.

"Shhhhh," said Ralph to Jan.

After a few sips, Dee looked at Jan. "Tell me all you know about these witch hunters. They are not nice people."

Ralph winced. "Oh my." Then he cleared his throat.

"Ummmm." Dee sipped and looked at him.

"Some of Randy's folk took the bodies away. We think that between fingerprints and the stuff they had in their pockets we should know who they are, ummm, who they were, pretty soon."

Dee nodded.

She looked at Jan.

He stared at her. "I already told you all that I know, which is not much. Just that crazy lecture and those guys chasing me. One of them was dumped in the dirt." He pointed at the spot and took a gulp from his glass. "Who are you? Really?"

Dee looked at Ralph.

He shrugged. "Jan is a free-lance newspaper reporter."

"No," stated Dee firmly. "Writing about us and all that you have seen for some people newspaper would be very not nice."

"Oh dear," said Ralph. Jan looked at him.

"I'll explain, ah, later." Ralph looked at Dee. "Dee?"

"As you heard, those not nice ones captured Ternala, the one in chains, and made her do not nice, telling her that they had her daughter and would only return her if she did as they told her. They didn't have her daughter."

Sandra refilled all their cups and removed the bottle from in front of Jan replacing it with one of the cups of coffee.

Dee sipped and then looked at Ralph.

"What?"

"The daughter of Ternala was found by one of the people."

Ralph jerked.

"Just so," said Dee.

Washington, D.C.

F. Fred stood, leaned across his desk, and shook her hand. "Congresswoman." And stared at her companion.

"Sit, Fred," said Sally Anderson as she dropped into one of the chairs. "You remember, S.A.?"

F. Fred plopped down and nodded. "I do."

"Pay close attention," added Sally. "She has a very

interesting proposal which I think you will find quite intriguing."

She leaned back and watched his face as S.A. carefully explained and handed over sheets covered with the facts and figures.

"I think that J. Robert would be interested as well," S.A. concluded. And stood. "I will leave you to discuss things in private. Shall we meet in a week?"

F. Fred nodded and looked at Sally.

"A week would be fine," she said. "I will contact J. Robert."

Maryland.

The two couples met in the home of Charles and Prentice. Randy and Anabelle had a baby-sitter for their twins. Richlin, their host's daughter, was at one of the many movie theaters.

Charles refilled his glass and shook a few grains of salt onto the thick foam and nodded at Randy.

Randy nodded back.

"That corporation that was being rebuilt that we discussed," Randy began.

"Uh huh," said Charles.

"That group has reorganized themselves. Now it is the same three politicians but only one of the corporations instead of the original two. It appears that the group has had second thoughts and are now headed in a different direction."

"Sounds good," said Charles.

Randy smiled. "That other corporation representative needs a very close looking into. The new group appears to not trust him."

Prentice smiled at Randy. "You know something?"

Randy shrugged. "A hunch."

Anabelle looked at the others. "The person, in that corporation of interest, is Franklyn," she spelled it for them, "Haberston."

"And?" said Charles.

"Haberston is known as one who, ah, bends the rules badly."

Charles nodded. "O.K."

"And," she continued, "he seems to have some rather peculiar friends, umm, associates, ah, as long as they have sufficient cash or will accept sufficient cash."

Charles smiled, a broad, happy smile. "I'll take care of it."

Florida.

It was an uninspiring building.

It was an unimposing office.

Both of these things suited the owner and operator of a very specialized business. He and his staff were very well paid to do what they did. But it was just a very good idea to not flaunt their true economic state of being. Customers that might visit could get the wrong idea.

He answered the phone on the first ring. This phone was a soft green, the color of money. He had changed it. It was as secure a phone as any phone could be made.

To call him on that phone cost the person on the other end quite a bit, just for the phone call. But then, those who would call could pay for the call.

"Yes?" He waited, pencil in hand, stack of paper sitting there, ready for whatever sort of notes he might take. It was a very thin stack, just a few sheets, destined to go up in a puff of smoke in a minute or two after he hung up.

"Ah," he said. "Oh! It is you."

"Ummm."

"I see."

"You want to do this right away?"

"Of course. Call me in one week."

He hung up, re-read his few notes, picked up the red phone and talked to the best of his best, and explained very carefully what the job was. "And the price is right." He laughed.

"You do realize that if you get caught it might be rather unpleasant?" He laughed. "Just making sure." He nodded to himself. "It will be in your account in a minute or two." He hung up. He hoped that they wouldn't be spotted. Of course, as far as he knew, they never had been.

Twisting to the side, he pulled up the correct screen on the large display, typed, and watched the money fly, electronically, from one place to another. Then he burned his notes in a special container.

Things Do Happen

House Darthar Na.

Dee was walking along the central hall on the second floor from her bedroom headed for the stairs down when she heard the soft singing.

She paused at the staircase leading up and started climbing toward the song. It was the first time she had heard singing since she had first started living in her house.

On the floor occupied by the Fontala, the warriors called The Protectors of The Innocent, she stopped and stared. They were all in the hall, drifting silently in the same direction, the direction of the song.

As she drew close to the open door, the meeting room of the Seventh Stand, there being seven stands to the Fontala, she stopped and peered in through the door at the group inside.

The male voices were all pitched to a low register singing a song so sad that she could feel tears starting to form. Over this floated the female voices, high pitched, clear notes like those struck from a crystal bell , singing a lament happy in a way that sent an understanding that all was not just sad and longing.

She turned to one of the Fontala, standing there, so still and listening.

"What is this song?"

He bowed to her. "Word," he said addressing her by

the term that meant the head of the Fontala. "This is a lament for the fallen. The song has not been heard since the very long ago."

"What fallen?"

A tear trickled over and down his cheek. "The very long ago lost Seventh Stand. Some of the members of the other Stands remembered parts and between them they helped the new Seventh Stand re-create the song. Soon all the Fontala will know it although the song is The Seventh Stand's. It has always been sung by the Seventh Stand of the Fontala, once every people year, for all our members who have perished doing their duties for the Feyra."

She bowed to him. "When all are done, tell the First Hand of each stand I wish to speak with them. Please."

"As the word says, so it will be done." He bowed.

Washington, D.C .

Two weeks had passed before they had finally found a time when they could meet.

So they did. In a very discreet room in a very discreet restaurant, they met. The four of them.

It was after dinner before they finally turned to the business of interest to them.

Sally Anderson looked around the table and nodded to them: F. Fred, J. Robert, and S. A.

S. A. handed each of them a folder. Each folder contained four pages. It was a very concise and to the point presentation. There was no wiggle room to spare for political buts or ifs or howevers. She waited for them to read it, and reread it, as necessary, and for them to look up. Her boss, Henry, had agreed. Commit to the project or leave. She refilled her teacup and took a sip.

Sally looked up first and smiled.

That's one, S. A. said to herself.

J. Robert looked up and nodded.

That's two, she thought. Now for the big kahuna.

F. Fred closed the folder, looked up, cleared his throat, realized that the others were waiting, and saw from their expression that they had agreed.

"Sure," he said. "Looks good. I can start tomorrow. I have two committee meetings."

Maine.

They were eating hamburgers, potato salad, and all the other things necessary to make hamburgers the treat that they were.

Sandra, helped by Jan, a rare occurrence for Sandra in accepting help at food preparation, had everything well in hand when, as he always seem to do, Charles drove up in his truck, parked, threw the driver door wide, jumped down, grinning broadly.

Ralph introduced Jan while Charles laced his hamburger with hot chili slices and other things before taking a large bite.

"Jan is our guest, " explained Sandra. "For a while."

"Okay." Charles took another chomp out of his burger.

Jan ate some of his potato salad and wondered who this big jock was.

When they finished, Charles and Ralph walked into the woods, on the game trail, to have a talk.

Charles sat on a handy stump, an ancient remnant from the logging in the area many years before, and frowned at Ralph.

"What?" Ralph leaned against a nearby pine tree, the lowest branches just above his head.

"Those three dead guys belonged to a group of real religious nuts. Their church is called The Flaming Sword of Truth Church Militant. They think they are some modern form of the Knights Templar and are paranoid about witches."

"Oh, dear," said Ralph.

Charles' eyebrows shot up. "Why are we interested in this particular batch of ding bats?"

"Things do twist around," sighed Ralph.

Charles grinned. "Okay, Ralph. What have you gotten us into this time?"

"I am not sure. Yet. But."

"Yes?"

"I think, without any evidence, yet, that they might have killed Sandrel's real parents."

Charles bounced to his feet. "I will have some of my sneaky types look into that crowd. If they can be linked to something like that, they will be in a world of hurt."

Jan watched the pair walk from the woods. Charles jumped into the truck and hurtled down the road. For a pair of folk on vacation, at the end of the narrow dirt road, these two certainly seemed, to him, to have a lot of visitors coming and going. Some of them were really peculiar.

Washington, D.C.

Randy opened the envelope and spilled out a report and a number of photographs. The envelope had been sent directly to him, no return address, postmarked locally.

So he read it. Slowly. Carefully.

The report detailed a number of meetings, here and there, between Franklyn Haberston and James James.

James James was the main subject of the photographs with most of them showing both men together in various locations. Randy made notes in the margin of the report.

The section on James Jame's was quite short, the gist of the report saying, so far, details were hard to come by.

Randy pushed one of several buttons and handed everything to the pair who walked in. They took the report and the photographs and left. They knew what was needed.

Randy wondered if that Corporation had any idea of what Franklyn was up to and with whom.

Florida.

It was an uninspiring building.

It was an unimposing office.

Both of these things suited the owner and operator of a very specialized business. He and his staff were very well paid to do what they did. But it was just a very good idea to not flaunt their true economic state of being. Customers might get the wrong idea if they ever chose to visit.

He answered the phone on the first ring. This phone was a soft green, the color of money, the color that money was at the moment. It was as secure a phone as any phone could be made.

To call into him on that phone cost the person on the other end quite a bit, just for the phone call. But then, those who would call could pay for the call.

"Yes?" He waited, pencil in hand, stack of paper sitting there, ready for whatever sort of notes he might take. It was a very thin stack, just a few sheets, destined to go up in a puff of smoke in a minute or two after he hung up. Then he sighed and wondered whether it was really worth running this business after all. He had called again.

"Ah," he said.

"Ummm."

"I see."

"Are you sure that you want to do this? With that group?"

"Absolutely! Call me in one week." Then he thought that maybe he would stay in business. They did pay better than top dollar, and then some, for his services and those of his employees.

He hung up, re-read his few notes, picked up the red phone and talked to the best of his best, and explained very carefully what the job was.

"You do realize that if you get caught it could be rather unpleasant?" He laughed. "Just making sure." He nodded to himself. "It will be in your account in a minute or two." He hung up.

Twisting to the side, he pulled up the correct screen on the large display, typed, and watched the money fly, electronically, from one place to another. One of these days that group would be able to retire comfortably on the amount they were now earning. Then he burned his notes in a special container. He smiled, a soft quiet smile, and thought, if they do retire maybe he would do that as well.

House Darthar Na.

Dee was eating the first meal of the day, eating and talking quietly with her daughters, Tiela and Winala.

They had been discussing House Kaanatan. It was one step from extinction. Feyra houses located in among the people often had this problem as few of the Feyra were interested in having a crosstie with them.

Now House Kaanatan was down to two, a mother and her daughter, and the daughter had agreed to be The Anointed One to another house, House Sextet, now comprised of two of the people and their adopted daughter, a Feyra.

So they had been talking quietly about this matter and decided to talk with Karanly, the First Sister of House Darthar, to see if she had an idea of what to do.

Maine.

Stanton Handersal stood and stared out the large picture window, out and over their compound and smiled. They had prospered. They now owned forty acres. The houses of the congregation were dotted here and there. The containment building stood not far from this building. It had a special purpose. It was the dwelling for their finder of witches, a sturdy log structure about the size of a single car garage with no windows and a single door.

The church proper was the only multi-story structure in their compound with his offices on the top floor.

Stanton Handersal stood and stared out the large window in his office, out and over their compound and smiled. I have a dream, he thought, and laughed softly to himself. He had always liked that speech, a speech of liberation. It was his dream as well, to liberate all of the people from the evil intervention of the witches.

He nodded. Now here they were, a small community, a large beginning, the home of The Flaming Sword of Truth Church Militant.

Truly, he thought, they were on a holy mission and were blessed. Money had come from an unlikely source, who donated much and wished for little. But, one did render unto Caesar the few things that Caesar wanted when asked.

The congregation had grown, some. It was hard labor to find the few, the pure of heart, the strong in the understanding of their holy mission.

He nodded to himself. They would soon find another of those that they sought. It was their destiny.

Sandra went inside the cabin and walked back out with Dee.

Dee was wearing her author-on-tour clothes.

Jan stared. And smiled at her "Now I recognize you. You are D. Grant, the author. I've been to a few of your readings. Are you on a book tour?"

Dee smiled back and sat at the table. Ralph handed her a cup of coffee and waited.

Dee took a few sips and looked at Jan. "I need a favor, Jan."

"Sure." He smiled happily. "Something is better than just sitting around here?" He really wondered which of the other bedrooms she had been in and why he never saw her inside the cabin.

She nodded.

Ralph and Sandra were watching her carefully.

"Ahhhhh, okay," said Jan. "What?"

Dee pointed. "I want you to guide me down that trail to that town. Please?"

He swallowed loudly. "I am not anxious to get beat up."

Dee stood. "You'll be safe." She took Sandra to one side and spoke softly. "Purr Cat and Ms. Hyde are coming along. Jan won't see them even a little bit."

Sandra hugged her and whispered, "Be careful, Dee. I think that group is dangerous."

"Careful cautious," replied Dee.

They walked back to the table. "Ready, Jan?" asked Dee.

He slowly stood and looked at Sandra.

She nodded. "Just remember our little talk. Go with

Dee."

Off they went, Dee and Jan and the two Furleen who blended into their surroundings and who were walking parallel to them, drifting unseen and unheard through the forest.

And eventually, they walked into the small town. The sun was long set. The buildings, the street lamps, cast pools of light across the sidewalks and the few people walking the streets.

"Pick a good place to stay," said Dee. "I pay for everything."

Jan nodded.

They had spent the day talking about various of her books, and the characters in them. And then about Trail Running. Finally Jan had told her of the various happenings in and around the camp. As it became dark he assured her that she was safe as he knew this trail very well.

As he led her toward a small hotel, he asked, "Who are those people?"

"Who?"

"Ralph and Sandra."

"Friends."

"What do they do for a living?"

Dee shrugged.

Jan nodded at her shrug. "Figured that would happen."

"What?"

"You know, but you won't tell me, right?"

"Just so."

He led her into the place that he had picked. Dee paid for two rooms, told the clerk that they would bring their belongings later, after they ate, and asked for a good restaurant.

As they ate, Jan told her that he had seen another poster advertising one of those lectures about witches.

"Good," said Dee. "Show me where, I want to go."

He nodded. And then over dessert tried to dissuade her from going.

"I will be safe." She laughed. "Who's going to worry about an author of fiction such as that I write." She frowned at him. "You stay in your room. One of them might recognize you. Okay?"

Jan agreed, unwillingly, but he agreed.

As Dee settled in the back row, she certainly hoped that he would stay in his room. She just wanted to hear what these people had to say. When the clipboard was passed to her, she printed her name, *D. Grant*, and smiled to herself and thought, investigate that all you want.

The lecture was winding down. It seemed to her to be less lecture and more rant than anything. A hand gently touched her left shoulder.

"D. Grant?"

She looked over her shoulder. "Yes?"

"A few words in the Hall. Please?"

Dee stood and followed him out into the Hall.

"What?" she asked.

"Our Father Soul wishes to speak to you."

"About?"

"I do not know. Please come. It is but a short walk."

She nodded. "All right. How far?"

"A mile past the edge of town."

"Lead on."

They strolled over two blocks and down a narrow road

out of town and turned to the right and then finally down an even more narrow dirt road and into the great clearing inside the forest.

She could see high walls, which appeared to be twelve or fourteen people feet high, all wood, all heavy timbers.

"You live inside a fort?" She could roof tops poking up here and there as well as a tall structure rising above everything else.

"No. We value our privacy, that is all."

He pushed and the small gate next to the large one swung in.

He led her into an open space and what appeared to be a scattering of houses and toward the large structure, the one she had seen poking up.

"This way." He headed into the building and stopped at the staircase and pointed. "Up there all will be explained."

People are strange, she thought as she started up, very strange.

On the third floor she walked along the only hall toward the only door, stopped, and knocked.

"Enter," said someone.

She did and stopped just inside the room.

"What?" she asked.

He spun from the window and gestured at a chair.

"Sit. I wish a favor."

She sat. "Oh?"

"You are D. Grant, the author?"

"Just so."

He nodded and began to tell her of the Great Mission they were on. As he spoke he began to stride back and forth, gesturing, pausing, telling her the story in rolling tones.

She listened. Very strange, she thought. And very, very

dangerous.

He stopped orating. "We would like you to write our history!"

She smiled. "I write fiction."

"We have read your books, D. Grant, we have. You have a rare insight into the witches."

She stared at him. "I do?"

He nodded. "Indeed. We have decided. You will write our history!"

She shrugged. "I will have to ask my editor. I have a contract." She stood.

"Look out this window." He strolled over and pointed out and down as she walked over. "See that small building?"

She looked down. "Yes."

"You will stay in there until you agree."

"Not a good idea."

He spun away, stepped to his desk, yanked open the drawer, and pulled something out. And shot her.

Virginia.

James James sat at his desk in his well-equipped home office and thought about how fine it was to have the several computers, the several telephone lines, and the high-speed wireless antenna on the roof.

Then he began reading several reports at once, eyes jumping back and forth, and making notes on another report. He sighed. He had told Franklyn that it was a stupid idea. But Franklin's ego had overridden good sense.

Now he had to clean up the mess. He drew many lines and spirals down the edges of the report as he thought about the problem. Then he stopped. And smiled. One more time he would do this. Afterwards he would have a, ahhhhh, pointed discussion with Franklyn.

Washington, D.C.

Charles picked up the phone as he turned his computer off.

"Hi, Randy."

He listened and looked at a picture of a flower covered meadow on one wall as Randy told him. Friends of those three cheap thugs that had tried to snatch his daughter had been found in a mall in Virginia. Stuffed into a dumpster.

"And?" said Charles.

Randy told him that they were still checking other friends and associates of those three. He now had, at the moment, two nervous characters stashed in a safe house.

Maine.

Doma Sparta was very good at not being seen. It was a skill that his order had perfected over generations.

He had been observing that very strange meeting which those religious zealots preferred to call a lecture. His curiosity was aroused when one of their member escorted a young woman from the place, and down a side street.

So he drifted along well back and finally watched the man escort her into that peculiar looking, walled place.

Now he waited in deep forest shadow far around one side in a place where he could not be possibly be seen by anyone coming and going through that gate, and watched as a young man hid way over there and watched whatever it was that he was watching. Something this peculiar should be observed carefully, thought Doma. From the poster he had read it appeared that the group that lived inside these tall walls believed in witches, a very strange belief for this day and age.

He had sufficient food and water in the many pockets of his outer garment to allow him to observe for a few days.

Stranger and stranger, he thought, as he spotted a pair of additional observers situate themselves in the woods right next to where the road entered this cul de sac, a very large clearing in the woods.

Washington, D.C.

His phone rang. He snatched it up. "Yes?"

He leaned back in his chair, phone cradled between neck and shoulder, pulled a pad of paper onto his lap and grabbed up a pen.

"One more time." He took more notes and frowned at them. "Okay, stay close, watch that place, and don't get caught." He nodded. "I know."

Then he nodded. "This is very special."

He set the phone in its cradle and pulled a cell phone from a pocket and dialed.

Maine.

Ralph picked it up. "Hello. Oh, hi there, Charles. One moment." He handed the phone to her.

"Charles?" Sandra nodded, took a few notes, and hung up.

Ralph looked at her.

"Boy, do we have a problem." She quickly explained. And was gone.

Vermont.

She had just returned from that small project.

Now she was relaxing on her patio behind the house, watching the birds jump around. Her place was a little way out of town, fairly private, although her neighbors up and down the road knew when she was home and when she wasn't. It was a small town after all. They kept an eye on her place when she wasn't home.

The phone rang. She picked it up

"Yes?" She stirred her iced tea with a finger.

"This is a surprise. Charles, right?"

And licked her fingertip.

"Relaxing. What do you want? I just got home!"

She jerked upright.

"Okay. We will be there as fast as the speed limit allows."

She turned the phone off, back on and made two phone calls. Then she walked into the house, added a few additional items to her ready pack, snatched it up and walked into the garage.

As she passed one of her neighbors, she waved and honked her horn three times.

He waved back, and would watch her place until she returned.

House Darthar Na.

She ran down the hall, shouting.

Ar are stepped from a room. "Sandra?"

She quickly explained.

"This way, please." He hurried up the stairs.

On the correct floor, he hurried her along the corridor and into a large room.

Kitea, First Hand, head of the Seventh Stand of the Fontala , looked up and stared at them and frowned at her.

"Ummmmm," said Kitea, wondering why one of the people was here and why Ar had let her into the house.

Ar bowed to Kitea. "This is Sandra, a, ummm, special friend of Daliera."

Sandra hurried over and sat down. And waited. A proper amount of time, barely contained.

"Dee was taken by some religious nuts two days ago to a walled compound they have. She hasn't come out." Then she explained, all that she knew, based on what Jan had told them before he and Dee had left to visit that small town.

Kitea nodded, spoke softly to the male sitting ever so quiet next to her, and watched as he hurried away. Then she looked at Ar. "We need Jonathon." And at her. "Go back, Sandra. And wait."

Sandra nodded, stood, and went home.

Jonathon walked in and looked at Kitea and the Seventh Stand assembling in the room, wearing their purple jackets and carrying their staffs which glowed a soft purple light. They called these staffs, Flaming Swords. They could cut through most anything. In the very long ago they had been crafted by Zanta the Clever of House Darthar.

He sat and sipped from the cup handed to him by Kitea.

She explained.

Maine.

Sandra walked from the cabin, coffee pot in hand, and poured a cup for herself, then one for Ralph.

"We are about to have a lot of company, dear."

"Oh," said Ralph

"Charles told me that a couple of his people saw Dee get kidnaped. They thought she was just visiting, except that she has been inside this fortified compound for two days. They also said that they saw Jan hiding in the woods watching the place as well."

Jonathon and the Seventh Stand stepped from the shadows at the edge of the forest. Jonathon walked over to the table with Kitea. They both sat. Ralph and Sandra handed filled cups to each of them.

Ralph nodded and smiled. "Hello, Jonathon."

Jonathon nodded, took a sip. "Can you show us on a map where this people place is located from here?"

Ralph stood. "One moment." He walked inside the cabin and returned, unfolding a map as he came. Spreading it on the table, he marked with a red *X* their cabin location and then drew a circle around the town. He pointed toward the forest. "That way."

Jonathon looked at Kitea.

"As soon as it is dark," she said, standing and walking over to the group standing and talking in small clusters, watching their surroundings.

Ralph tapped the circle on the map. "Dee felt that group was not nice."

"Ummmmm." Jonathon took a sip.

"Charles has a couple of people in the area, just watching. The place is about a mile from town to the east in an isolated setting with a high wooden wall around it. Another bunch will arrive shortly. To watch as well."

"Ah," said Jonathon, taking a sip.

"I want to come," said Sandra. "May I?"

Jonathon stood. "Stand up."

She did.

He grabbed her upper arms and lifted her off the deck and held her suspended. Then he set her down. "It can be done."

Maine.

Her eyes fluttered and opened and slowly focused.

She had a bad taste in her mouth.

One small light was on, just illuminating the room.

She rolled her head to one side and looked at the woman slumped in the only chair, sleeping.

"You!" she rasped

The woman stirred.

"WAKE UP!"

She jerked awake.

"Oh. You're awake."

"Just so. Water."

She bounced up and filled the only glass on the small table from the only pitcher.

Dee sat up and took the glass, tasted the water, then emptied the glass.

"You drugged me?"

She nodded.

"How long?"

"Two days."

Dee yanked at her bindings. "Chains?"

"It was so decided."

"You think that drugging me and binding me in chains is the way that will get me to write your history?"

"Our Father Soul said that in this way that you would learn to do as he wishes."

"That was truly a big mistake. Can you take a message to him? Now?"

She nodded.

"Tell him that he is not nice, his house is not nice, and I will be released immediately."

She shook her head. "It will not happen."

Dee picked up the pitcher and drink from it, emptying it. Then she stood and yanked at her chains.

"Release me."

"No."

"Then I will."

The woman stared at her. The captive suddenly began shimmering, fading in and out. Some other shape was beginning to appear. She screamed, yanked open the door, charged though it, bolted the door shut from the outside and ran into the central structure.

Ziaza was in constant contact with her group, now comprised of team one and team two. Each team had a leader who was linked to all their team members. She was linked to the leaders. They reported every 10 minutes, or sooner if something required it.

Her entire crew was inside the forest, hidden in deep shadow. They were watching that compound and were evenly spaced around it. The folk in there had cleared a hundred foot wide swath all around the place.

She was in voice contact with Charles via secure radio. Charles and her team leaders heard everything that she or Charles said.

"So far, so good. Very quiet."

It was late at night, clear sky and moonless, and it seemed that the inhabitants inside the compound were sound asleep, as one would expect. She straightened up and stared up into the black.

"Charles, have you sent in paratroops of some kind?"

"Then who are they. They're reported coming down all around the place using some new form of parachute." She snorted. "They are carrying long poles that seem to glow with a soft purple light."

"What! Say again!"

She started to run for the exit, the place where the road came into the large opening. "Everyone out! Now! Now! Now!"

Jan hurtled down the road after them. He had been sneaking through the forest back to town to eat, then returning to this spot to watch the place and the other people out there doing the same thing. This was getting really weird.

He ran through the mob and jogged easily next to the woman, obviously their boss.

"Did Dee get out?"

"No," she gasped. "No one came out of that place."

"D. Grant, the author. They took her in there. And she has not come out." He was breathing easy as this jog was a walk in the park for him.

"No idea. Have no idea who that is." she stopped, sucked in deep breaths, and spun around. "And who are you?"

They were far down the road. The group reorganized itself inside the woods.

"Jan. I was watching Dee when she went inside that place."

Ziaza looked through special goggles back at the compound. "Whoever they are, Charles, no one can get in or out through that gate."

She almost dropped the things.

"Charles, speak to me! What is going on? I just saw what looked like a gigantic bat settle to the ground. It was carrying a woman who was holding a gun. Now it isn't there! Just some guy and that woman with the gun. Is this some kind of crazy military operation going on?"

Inside the holding structure Dee shifted and altered. The chains snapped as she began to occupy most of the space in the small cabin. She had spent days and days in hard training with Ar learning this unique skill. She had argued long and hard to convince him to do it. He was afraid she wouldn't be able to control it when she was that way, driven out of control by that great hunger, but she had learned the skill and the necessary control. Jonathon had argued that no other Feyra should ever learn this house skill. Dee had agreed.

She arched her back, great hind legs pushing up.

The roof cracked and exploded, pieces flying into the air, scattering across the open space, bouncing off the nearby structure.

The Karthan reared up, eyes glittering red in the faint light. It was the gigantic ancient female predator form of the Feyra.

The Karthan dated from the very long ago when the Feyra were only small roaming families and the people were few and far between and barely using tools. That form, then and now, would frighten anything alive.

In the present time the Karthan shape only occurred when the females were about to have children. They were locked and bolted inside specially built and heavily constructed rooms capable of containing them for the short time required as the great hunger they felt from the birthing process now made them ravenous beyond control. It was that lack of control that Dee had mastered. A Karthan burned up great quantities of energy just existing.

Any Feyra seeing one of them on the loose would flee for their lives if they did manage to escape.

Any of the people who saw one would run screaming and wondering how such a large predator looking like something that had escaped from the age of dinosaurs could possibly be here in this day and age.

The Karthan were immense creatures with thick and long rear legs, long arms, a long neck, a elongated face and skull, all limbs ending in large claws. It was a sight to cause nightmares.

Great teeth and fangs snapped in anger as she kicked one wall out and stalked over to the main building and began to climb up the outside wall toward the large window on the third floor.

Ziaza gasped. "Charles! Pieces of roof structure just flew up into the air. No explosion that I could hear!"

She sucked in a deep breath. "You won't believe this! What looks like a prehistoric monster is climbing up the outside wall of the main building. Those paratroops are all running into the forest. And we are leaving. Right now!"

She spun and pointed. Her crew raced down the road, headed for town, and to where they had parked their vans.

Jan hurtled in a different direction.

Dee smashed in the large window of Stanton's office and ripped a great opening in the wall through which she thrust her head and one arm.

Dragging him out, long talons wrapped around his middle, she climbed up to the roof and perched near one edge.

"So, little piece of meat," she hissed. "You would drug me and keep me prisoner to write the history of your nonsense."

Stanton Handersal howled. A demon from the worst nightmare imaginable had him.

"Shhhh," she growled. She shook him, rag doll flopping

back and forth. "Don't you like it? You killed many of my folk, burned their house down." One glittering red eye stared at him from the great head. "Maybe I shall just eat you." A long rough tongue rasped over his cheek, tearing the skin.

He stared and screamed, "Monster spawn of hell, who sent you?"

"You were told it was not a good idea to hold me. I didn't like being shot with that electrical thing or being drugged." She gave him another shake.

He gasped, eyes flying wide. "You?"

"You and your group are very not nice. Payment is due for all the abuse and the destruction and death that you gave so freely."

Rearing up on her great hind legs, she threw him howling up and out into the dark night.

Stanton smashed through the roof of a nearby house. Frightened people ran from the rubble and stared upward with disbelieving eyes. She leaped. Scattering the remains of the house and its inhabitants in all directions, she bounced away and smashed the main gate into the open space outside the compound.

"No one leaves," she hissed to the two Furleen standing there. "No one."

She leapt over them and stood outside the compound. And collapsed into herself. Soon she would have to rest and eat a number of large meals.

"Come," she called. "The Fontala have work to do."

Doma Sparta slipped deeper and deeper into the forest. Then he hurried on a curving arc that would eventually lead out into the nearby town.

He stepped into the first hotel, took a room, locked the

door, and began to write page after page of everything that he had seen or heard in his pocket journal. When he was finished, he sat and stared at the wall.

Tomorrow he would return to New Mexico and compare what he had seen to those things mentioned in their most ancient writings.

Washington, D.C.

Randy charged into Charles' office.

"You won't believe it!"

Charles took a sip of black coffee. He had been drinking a lot of it this evening. "What?" He hooked the headset off his head and set it next to one of the phones.

Randy dropped into a chair

"We just sent a team via fast helicopter to a small town in Maine. The locals reported a terrorist attack on some church group outside of town. Our team is in place and reporting."

"You're kidding?"

Randy shook his head.

"Photos will be sent soon. Hard to believe, what they said via secure transmission."

"What?"

"Kindling. Every structure is kindling but the tallest. No fire. It is like William Williams the Third's place all over again. Every piece of paper gone. Every computer is without hard drives and cut into pieces. My guys say that one small structure next to the tall one appears to have exploded but they can't find any trace of explosions. Another house appears to have had a body fall from a great height through the roof. They think that the remains are the head guy from what I.D. they found but can't explain how he could do something like that. The great gates were blown off their hinges to the outside, not from the outside. That, like lots of other things, doesn't make a whole lot of sense."

"Any survivors?"

"Two. Shocked into crazy, crying about demons and dark angels."

Charles smiled. "Demons and dark angels. Sounds pretty crazy alright." He looked at his watch. "Time to go home, sleep till noon. I've had a long night. When can I see the photos?"

Randy stood. "They'll be on your desk by the time you come in." He hurried out the door.

Charles locked his office and headed home. He wondered what kind of paratroops those really where.

Maine.

Sandra stumbled into the cabin and banged all the lights on, every one of them.

Ralph charged from their bedroom, gun in hand, stopped, and stared at her.

"What?" He set the gun on a table and walked over to her. "What?" She didn't look good.

Sandra collapsed into his arms. "Hold me, Dear, just hold me."

Then she told him. Finished, she stepped back and over to make a pot of coffee in the coffee maker.

He watched her. "Nothing stronger?"

"I'll put it in my coffee." She walked to the couch and dropped into it.

He joined her, holding two glasses and a bottle. "Just a wee bit, first?" He tipped a splash into each glass, and handed her one.

She took a sip. "Dear?"

"Yes." He poured a little more into her glass.

"I left out a whole lot."

"O.K."

She leaned against him. "No one would ever believe it if I told them what I saw, which I won't, of course. Ever!"

"O.K."

She held out her glass. "Let's skip the coffee."

"O.K." He poured a lot into her glass.

She took a long swallow. "They are the most dangerous folk we have ever met, anywhere."

He slipped an arm over her shoulders, set his glass down, took her's as she finished and set it on the table, and held her until she fell asleep.

"I know."

New Mexico.

Doma Sparta sat in the silence of their library, slowly reading through a handwritten manuscript. He had been doing this for three days, searching for any mention of what he had seen.

He had started at the beginning, at the slim volume that had started their order.

From what he had seen of them, their clothes were dark, but so were their wings. At least, in the darkness of the moonless night, they appeared to have wings, dark wings of some new sort of design of military parachute. The military was always developing such new and interesting things.

He stared at yet another page, telling him nothing useful, nothing at all. Doma sighed. What he had seen, he had seen.

Then he laughed, mostly at himself, but a little at his order. His mind had once again given him a different idea. One he wasn't about to share. The order, they called themselves "Searchers," had been searching in all the wrong places for all that time, generations of time looking for angels and demons.

Angels and Demons and all of that ilk were creatures of the human imagination. They had been searching for their own figments of their own imaginations.

He stood and walked from the library. This was a waste of time. It was time to revisit that small town in Maine and then start an entirely new type of search.

Washington, D.C.

Charles was shuffling paper, which is how he viewed the need to do what he was doing. It was the one aspect of his job that he really and truly hated. However, some of this stuff he couldn't hand to his staff to do.

A phone buzzed. He picked it up, happy for the interruption. "Yes?" He nodded. "Sure. Send her in."

He shoved all the papers into a folder, stuffed the folder into the appropriate drawer, locked the drawer, leaned back in his chair, and watched the door to his office.

It was a few minutes walk to his office from the front desk.

And in a few minutes the door was opened by a tall man. "Go right in." He stepped back and waited.

She strolled in, sat in a handy chair, and glared at him.

Charles nodded as the door closed. "Yes?"

"What exactly went on out there?" Ziaza scowled at him.

He leaned further back in his chair and watched her face.

"Well?" she demanded.

He shrugged.

"Bull!" she snapped.

He nodded.

And laughed. "But true." He held up his hands. The fingers on the right hand splayed out. The other hand had all but one finger curled tight.

She lurched to her feet. "Secret handshake?" she snapped.

"No. That is how many people know anything at all about what you're wondering about. You are not one of those six."

She glowered at him. "I can't work this way! I will not put my people in a crazy situation like that ever again! We are not interested in getting into the middle of some night time military raid with freaky things going on!'"

"SIT!"

Slowly she did, glaring at him.

He watched her face. "Not one word, ever, to anyone. Promise?"

She nodded, slowly. "Okay."

"Any leak and you will wish for something more comfortable, like a jail in some poor country south of our border. Still okay?"

"Yes," she hissed, and relaxed, some, and leaned back in her chair.

"You have heard of The Council, no doubt."

She nodded.

"There are six members only one of whom is known or recognized."

"Fredrickson," she said. "He and his wife died."

He nodded. And winked. And smiled at her. She jerked back in her chair and stared at him. He laughed. "By sticking my neck way out there, this time, I think I can arrange for you to communicate with the dead. A sort of private séance."

She laughed. "Bad joke, Charles."

"No joke."

"Ahhhh, what obligation does this put me in? This time? You are already pulling my strings and jerking me and my people around."

"That won't change."

"Then what?"

"Let's just say that perhaps a little information might make what you do, ahhhh, more interesting."

He stood. "Ready?"

So did she. "For what?"

"Let's take a drive."

A Very Large Place.

They stood by the small door built into the very large door. The building was constructed of large, dark stone, with pediments and towers all along the upper walls.

He stepped up and gently knocked on the small door set in the very large door and stepped back.

They waited.

Finally the small door swung inward.

A very large and thick in every direction figure stood in the obscuring gloom inside.

"What do you want?" snarled the shape.

Aradon bowed to him. "Here is Aradon and here is Fratl of House Ranadan, come to visit." They both bowed.

The person stepped into the light.

They tried not to stare.

Bright yellow eyes peered at them over a long muzzle, white canines poked down past the lower jaw.

"House Ranadan?" he growled.

"Just so," replied Aradon.

"Do come in, Aradon and Fratl." He spun and walked into the interior and led them down a long hall into a large room and dropped into massive chair and waved them to two others. Now he looked like most any of The Feyra.

As they sat, Hongor bounced up, grabbed a large steaming vessel and filled two green mugs. He handed one to each, filled another, and sat, and took a sip. "What?"

"We would like to know the total history of House Mataraen as far back as you have records. Please." Aradon took a sip. It was quite good.

Maine.

The large pickup charged up the long dirt road and parked at the end of the sorta rambling log cabin. The dust cloud drifted into the forest.

The doors flew open and he jumped out.

"Oh boy," laughed Charles. "What's for dinner?"

"Grilled chicken, Charles. We have plenty." Sandra smiled at him.

Ralph and Sandra watched her leave the pickup and walk around the end and slowly come their way. Doubt and disbelief cycled across her face.

"Brought a guest for dinner," announced Charles, sitting at the table and pouring his glass full from a handy can just placed there by Sandra. He stared at her. "You look beat, really really beat."

Sandra nodded. "Just tired, very, very tired." And watched the woman carefully approach.

Ralph smiled at her and looked at Sandra. "Sandra, this is Ziaza. She and her group were watching me, some, once."

Sandra hurried into the cabin and then back. "Here.

Plates, forks, etc. Sit down. Have some dinner." She poured a glass of red wine and set it next to Ziaza's plate.

As they ate, Charles looked around.

"Jan and Dee went home," said Sandra.

Charles topped up his glass, sprinkled a few grains of salt on the thick foam, and took a drink.

"Jan," explained Sandra, "is going to write an article, or two, about those religious witch hunters."

"A reporter!" gasped Ziaza. She glowered Charles.

Ralph nodded. "He stayed out here for a while. We talked about, ah, things."

Charles winked at Ziaza.

They had ice cream for dessert, vanilla. Charles dumped a bunch into his glass and poured the rest of the large can over it.

"Beer float. Really quite good. Read about it somewhere."

"You're the double," stated Ziaza looking at Ralph and wondering about Charles. "What are you doing way out here?"

Charles laughed.

Ralph looked at him.

"It's all right, Ralph. Ziaza has a special, let's call it, relationship, with me. She and her crew and that guy down in Florida."

Sandra added more ice cream to Ralph's bowl. "Finish it."

Ralph did. And licked his lips.

"We," he said to Ziaza, "are not doubles. We are not dead. We are not ghosts."

He nodded. "But for a while, we are still dead as far as the world is concerned."

"You run The Council," said Ziaza.

"Just so." Ralph smiled. It was a response he had picked up from listening to Dee and Jonathon.

"Who's Dee?"

"D. Grant, the author."

Sandra nodded, adding a little more red wine to her glass and Ziaza's.

Ziaza took a sip of her wine, "You know her?" It was the person that Jan had said was trapped inside that walled compound.

"A friend," said Sandra.

Ziaza looked at Charles, then at Ralph and Sandra. "Oh."

Ralph watched her carefully as she was looking just a little faint.

"Am I safe?" whispered Ziaza. "Or am I going to disappear?"

"Perfectly safe," stated Ralph. "A very strange thing to worry about."

Ziaza looked at Charles. "True?"

"Yep." He emptied his glass.

Sandra walked in the cabin and back out again and handed Charles another large cold can.

"I really need a bunch of time off," sighed the Ziaza.

"You could stay with us," offered Sandra. "We have room."

"We are on a vacation," added Ralph.

A Problem. Or Two.

House Darthar Na.

Dee, Karanly, and Ternala walked into one of the small comfortable rooms with a large outside window. Dee served them coffee, took her cup, sat in one of the comfortable chairs, sipped and waited.

Karanly and Ternala did the same thing, waited. It was a most polite thing to do so.

Dee nodded, after the proper amount of time had passed. "Here is Karanly, First Sister of House Darthar. Here is Ternala, Head of House Kaanatan. The First Daughter of House Kaanatan has agreed to be The Anointed One of House Sextet, the home of her adopted parents. She made that decision before she knew that her mother was still alive. Now House Kaanatan is none but Ternala."

Karanly gasped.

Dee looked at her. "House Kaanatan was almost eliminated by an organization of very not nice people."

Karanly frowned, then glared at her. "They must pay for such!"

"Just so." Dee nodded. "They are no more. Speak with Jonathon."

Karanly nodded and took a sip. "Ah ummmm."

Dee nodded. And waited.

Someone soft knocked on the door to the room.

"Enter," said Dee.

She entered and looked at the trio seated there. Dee handed her a filled cup and looked at Ternala. "Here is Winala, Second Daughter, The Anointed One of House Darthar Na. She is studied deep in all Feyra House important matters. She will bring much to our discussion and planning."

She took a sip and watched Ternala. "If the House Head wishes to carry her house forward."

Ternala sipped and nodded, struggling to keep her face composed.

Then the discussion started and wandered long into the day. Ternala stressed that her house skills were mainly in crafting three-dimensional art and that she would require a house location either inside a people cluster or not too far away. Then she stood, walked to the window, and stared outside, and whispered, "The House now has no skills trainer, all that knowledge of our house skills has been lost in the destruction."

Dee looked over as the door opened and Ar walked into the room. He looked at the group and then at Dee. "Princess?"

"Sit, please."

He did, carefully. It was most unusual to do that, for one of his kind.

She watched his face. "When House Kaanatan was being destroyed what happened to their skills trainer?"

Ar sighed heavily. "With the house structure destroyed and the only two survivors widely scattered, that one would be either hidden deep, or . . . "

"Ah ummmmm," said Dee softly.

Ar looked at her and reached out and pulled.

Sandrel stumbled in and gasped. "OUCH!"

"Most sorry," said Ar.

Dee looked at Ar.

He stood and turned. "Sandrel, do you have something from the day when you were found by the people?"

She stared at him.

Dee stood and handed Sandrel a filled cup. "Join us." She waggled her hand at an empty chair.

Sandrel sat, took a sip, and carefully searched each face. "An ornate brooch was pinned to my clothes. But I never wear it. Too fancy."

Ar nodded. "Do you have it here?"

She shook her head. "I keep it in a small box at home."

Dee nodded.

Sandra walked in. "Dee? Oh, hello, ummmmm, everyone."

Dee smiled at her. "Here is Sandra, mate of Ralph, Head of House Sextet. Here is Karanly, First Sister of House Darthar."

Karanly stared at Sandra and frowned. "One of the people? How can she do that?"

Dee lightly touched Karanly's arm. "It is a House Darthar Na secret. We will talk later."

Karanly nodded and took a sip.

Dee looked at Sandrel. "Please tell Sandra how to find that box so that she can bring it here." She handed a thick folder to Sandra. "And give this to Charles."

Maine.

Sandra had cleared the table and walked into the cabin and soon returned, carrying a bulging expandable file folder. She handed it to Charles.

"What?" He refilled his mug from a cold can.

"Correspondence and economic forms of all sorts and things like that there."

He nodded. "O.K., it will get a thorough and careful study." He emptied his mug and looked across the table. "You going to stay out here for a few days?"

Ziaza nodded. "I think that I will."

Charles handed her a cell phone. "Gimme a call when you are ready to leave." He winked at her, stood, and walked over to his truck, jumped inside, and headed down the dirt road trailing a cloud of dust.

Washington, D.C.

Charles and Randy were eating in the cafeteria at Randy's organization.

"Pretty good," said Charles, taking another large bite from his hamburger.

Randy smiled. He was eating a large salad with all manner of things in it beside the greens.

Finally, as Randy sipped his tea and Charles worked on a large slice of peach pie, Randy said, "We have some new information from, ahhh, a loose acquaintance of those three dead thugs, the ones that tried for your daughter."

"Immmm," said Charles as he chewed.

"Swift Nicky Tanagal is willing to talk with us."

Charles swallowed and picked up his coffee container. After a few swallows from that, he said, "That is a surprise."

"He is being very careful. Wants us to meet him in a place up the coast in a house by the ocean in Massachusetts."

"When?"

"Couple of days."

"Sure." Charles smiled. "Just you and me?"

Randy nodded.

Charles laughed. "Sounds like fun."

Maine.

They had finished breakfast several days later, several days after Charles had left Ziaza to visit Ralph and "take a vacation."

Ralph poured some cream into his coffee and gave it a slight stir with a spoon just to watch the white swirl around in the black. Then he looked up. A mountain bike was coming up the long dirt road trailing a small plume of dust.

It coasted up to the porch and Jan climbed off.

"Morning," He smiled at Sandra.

"Pull up a chair. I'll get you some breakfast."

He stepped up onto the deck, sat at the table, and looked across it. "Jan," he said.

"Ziaza," she replied. "You the reporter." Her lips almost curled on that last word. She nodded. "I remember you."

Jan nodded. "Only a little bit of a reporter. You do?"

She smiled. "At that walled compound near that small town."

"Jan," explained Ralph, "is a Trail Runner of some repute and spends most of time doing that."

Ziaza took a hard look at him. "Really?"

"Yep." Jan poured his cup full from the pot on the table.

Sandra plopped down a dish heaped with potatoes, sausage, and scrambled eggs, shoved it over to Jan, and then a knife and a fork. "There you go." She sat. Ralph refilled her cup.

"How did the article go?" asked Sandra.

"Lots of interest," said Jan around a mouthful. "Religious nuts are always of interest. Especially if there are articles about them being terrorists of a zealous nature and all that."

Ziaza looked at Ralph.

He nodded. "They were the modern version of the bad old days in Salem, witch hunting and all that sort of thing, thought that they were The Knights Templar reincarnated."

Jan finished the last bit of the hash browns and filled his glass with orange juice. "Guess I won't have to worry about being chased by them through the woods any more."

"They chased you?" Ziaza refilled her coffee cup. "Why not?"

So Jan told her all about that, stressing that once he hit the trail inside the forest he was really quite safe, and how he came out right next to here and how Ralph and Sandra put him up for a couple of days.

Ralph looked at Ziaza. "They are dead. The whole bunch."

"What?"

"Their place was destroyed by persons unknown."

Ziaza looked at Ralph and wondered exactly what kind of military operation it was that she had seen and decided to change the subject. "So Jan was on vacation here as well?"

Ralph smiled at her.

Jan looked across the table. "So, what do you do, job and all that?"

"Oh." She smiled at him. "I watch people for a living."

"You do?"

"Uh huh." Her smile broadened. "How I met Ralph."

Washington, D.C.

They met in one of the many small meeting rooms in the sprawl of the government warren.

They were all there, politicians and corporation representative.

Around the table sat F. Fred and Jeramia, Sally

Anderson and Jons Whitehall, J. Robert Brown and his aid, Trina Weathera, and Sally Ann Dutog representing Henry A. Ansen and the Special Projects section of her corporation.

F. Fred rapped a knuckle on the table top and waited until he had all their attention.

"Ahem," he said. "We have a mutual problem which is going to cause some, ahhhh, effort to solve, some combined effort on all our parts to solve." Shoving a broad smile into place, he gazed around the table.

"What problem?" asked J. Robert. "Or should I ask, which problem?"

Sally poked him in the ribs with her elbow.

"A snake name Franklyn," said Jeramia.

"Snake indeed," agreed Sally. She looked at F. Fred. "Problem?"

"Ahem, ahem." F. Fred's smile wilted away. "He is still pursuing that organization which we all agreed was not, ahem, a good idea. Ahem, it will complicate our own plans if not put them into jeopardy."

"Oh, yes," agreed Sally Ann. "Definitely a problem."

"Well, S. A.," said The Congresswoman. "Whatever he wants, I think that we have enough strings to pull to see that he won't get it, at least not from the government."

Massachusetts.

It was one of the older but well maintained houses. It was perched on a high spot near the shore. As Charles climbed from his truck, he could see a number of large men wearing wind-breakers wandering here and there around the building.

"Guess Swift Nicky is at home," he said as Randy walked around the truck and joined him. "Shall we go see what he has to say?"

Randy nodded and headed for the door.

Charles smiled and followed. "He does seem to be rather nervous about something."

"Can't be us." Randy thumped on the door.

The door swung in and two more of the wind-breaker clad men waved them inside. Another beckoned them to follow him.

As they stepped into the large living room, Charles laughed. "Honey, I'm home!"

Swift Nicky Tanagal, lounging in a chair, dressed in very casual attire that reeked of money, smiled at Charles and waggled one hand at the other two chairs. "Please sit."

Charles dropped into one. Randy inspected the other, then sat.

"A number of bodies have been turning up," said Swift.

"Right," agreed Charles.

Swift looked at him. "What do you know?"

"Three religious nuts and six hoods are the ones we are, or were, ah, interested in," stated Charles. "Any other carcasses turning up don't count."

Swift nodded. "Some of those nine are linked to a certain airplane crash and some are linked to something else."

Randy watched him very carefully. Charles idly looked at everything in the room.

"And?" asked Charles, looking up at the ceiling.

"From what I have heard, all the money that they needed came from the same source even if the players are, umm, different."

Charles sat up. He had been comfortably slouching. "Are you going to tell us?"

Swift nodded.

"How come?"

Swift sighed. "That source appears to be a potential problem for many people."

Charles grinned at him. "So, what do you have that would be informative and helpful?"

Swift nodded. One of the wind-breakers stepped over and handed Charles a thick folder.

"That folder contains copies of documents of various sorts. From there I believe that you will be able to back track and, ahhhhh, take appropriate action."

Charles set the folder in his lap. "And what do you want?"

"Nothing."

"Surrrrre . . ." drawled Charles.

"Charles," sighed Swift. "We have known each other since grade school, you, me, and Ralph." He shrugged. "So we happen to be on different sides of the fence. No matter." And leaned forward. "I take this as a personal affront, what is going on, this time."

He sat up, very straight. "This source wants to play outside of the rules, so to speak. This has become a problem!"

Swift stood, walked over, and set one hand on Charles' shoulder. "Let me know if you can't solve this problem." He gave the shoulder a squeeze, and nodded. "Take care, buddy. But wait a while before you leave." As he headed for the door, he laughed. "See ya!"

Randy stood and walked over and looked out one of the windows at the ocean. "Charles, tell me about your grade school."

Charles stepped up to his side. "Not much to tell." Then he told him. "This is how we met, a small school in a small town in New Hampshire."

New Hampshire.

Charles had always been big for his age, regardless of whatever age he was. His father was a policeman so he had absorbed a view of good and bad that was mostly at variance with the view of most of his fellow students in the eighth grade in this small school in this small town.

His size and attitude and being one of the new students here set him aside from most of the others especially as he was too big to pick on, the fate of new students.

Standing to one side of the area utilized by the students for athletics and other outdoor activities, he watched his fellow students, spotted those guys who took on the bully role, and saw one of the other new students approaching.

"Hello," said the slightly build guy dressed in clothes that were better than that worn by anyone else, including the teachers. He had to look up.

"Hi," replied Charles. "I'm Charles." He reached out and shook the hand that was offered. This guy had a good grip.

"I am Swift Nicky Tanagal." He smiled and then explained that it wasn't a nickname but a given name. It was a family tradition to name the first born son in each generation that. There were no "juniors" or numbered Swifts. That was also a family tradition. These customs reached back for many generations. Then he explained that his parents had decided that for the betterment of his education that it was now required that he go to a public school. So here he was.

"Sure, Swift," acknowledged Charles. "Please to meet you."

And so as time wandered past them in the eighth grade they stood and talked, casually now and then, here and there.

Then on fine day while they stood talking outside in the activity field an event happened that created a bond between them.

Anderson Schmidt, a rather overweight but determined bully, who had been picking on Swift and making snide remarks about his name each and every day, stomped over to the pair, interrupting their conversation, accompanied by his three buddies, junior bullies in training, as it were.

The group had decided that it was time to up the amount of harassment that they gave to Swift regardless of who he might chose to talk to.

As they started in, Charles cleared his throat loudly.

The group looked at him.

"Knock it off," ordered Charles.

The four crowded around and close to Charles and began making rude comments.

So Charles punched Anderson in the face, breaking his nose, and happily thumped his associates.

Charles was sent home.

His father charged into the Principle's Office and got things settled.

From that day on, Charles and Swift were buddies and even helped each other with their homework, although in many cases it was a mutual struggle to complete certain assignments on time.

But in the ninth grade everything changed.

It was a sunny day in the fall not long after school had started and Swift and Charles were outside with all the others, talking quietly, when they spotted a new student, a rather thin but compact guy who walked past the junior league smart mouths, who were calling things at him, as if they didn't exist.

Charles smiled. He liked that guy's attitude.

The guy stopped, picked up one of the balls laying here and there, and tossed it at Charles.

He laughed when Charles, rather casually, reached out and caught it. And tossed it back.

That guy caught it, walked up to the pair and introduced himself, dropping the ball on the grass.

Charles laughed and pointed. "Don't worry about those guys."

"Who?"

Swift stared at him. "The ones with the big mouths standing over there."

"Oh." Ralph shrugged. He turned, looked here and there, and nodded.

"Ralph?" asked Charles.

Ralph turned back. "What?"

"Ahhhhh, Swift and I get together after school and work on our homework. You can join us. We'll help you get caught up."

Ralph smiled. "Thanks. But, ah, it really isn't necessary." He shrugged. "But I'll keep you company, if that is all right."

So they met every day after school to do homework. And two of the trio were shocked at what happened.

Ralph carefully explained whatever the assignment was and how to finish it. His explanations were better than any of the teachers giving the assignments. Swift and Charles quickly came to realize exactly how unusual their new companion really was.

And so it went, grade after grade, until graduation and afterwards.

It was at Swift's home for his graduation party from high school that Charles understood what Ralph had known for years but hadn't mentioned.

Swift's family business, or rather businesses, were the sorts of activities that Charles' father put folks in jail for doing, if it could be proven. Swift's family had a knack for not having things proven.

Charles was standing over at one side of the room next to the punch bowl refilling a large glass when Swift stepped up to him and looked up into his face. "Still friends?"

Charles emptied half the glass and nodded. "Still friends."

Ralph wandered up, munching on something, and looked at them. "What?"

Charles laughed, set his glass down, and hugged them, both at the same time. "Still friends." And laughed, a happy booming sound.

House Dartha Na.

Dee, Karanly, and Ternala were sitting, talking quietly when the pair opened the door to the small comfortable room with the large outside window and waited in the opening.

"Please do join us," said Dee.

They walked in.

Dee nodded and said. "Here is Dontilax, House Head of Antarax, a crafter house, and here is First Sister Zarpon. Their new house is located not too far from, not too close to, the large people place named Portland, Oregon. It is a large people cluster that appreciates the arts and crafts." She indicated the empty chairs, stood, and handed the pair filled cups.

And after the proper time had passed she explained that House Antarax made pottery. It was a stunning, thin-walled design of a deep luminescent green that had great appeal to the people. They made cups, bowls, platters, and dishes and sold them at various of the small markets and craft fairs around the area.

"It would be a nice place to locate House Kaanatan, a

crafter house of three-dimensional art." Dee smiled at Dontilax. "Here is Ternala, Head."

He bowed. "It would be our pleasure to help House Kaanatan."

Zarpon smiled at Ternala. "Just so. Come visit with us and then decide."

Ternala nodded.

House Ranadan.

They sat in a simply furnished room of four chairs and small tables, filled coffee cups in hand.

Anadaz took a sip and looked at them.

Aradon nodded. "That house is certainly an ancient line." He took a sip.

"Most wolf-like for a moment," added Fratl.

Anadaz smiled at them.

"He spend a long time in his library, searching," said Aradon.

"And growling," added Fratl. "Careful cautious, mother."

Anadaz stared at her. And took a sip.

Aradon took a sip and began. "House Mataraen was a Shadow House to House Narkalar, the house that threatened Daliera Fontala, and to House Energat, the one that had organized The Dark Nine Cluster, intending to rule over all the Feyra. It was during the time of the removal of The Dark Nine Cluster that the Seventh Stand of The Feyra was lost, all members died as did House Nagan of that cluster. In a great battle in that very long ago The Fontala eliminated House Energat and the great dark things that they had brought into existence. The Feyra then drew back to their home quarters to sleep and to heal."

"Ummmmmmm." Anadaz took a sip.

Fratl nodded. "A house skill of House Mataraen is called long sleep."

"Ahhhhhh. Perhaps I should visit House Darthar Na and speak with Daliera Fontala.

"Just so," said Aradon.

Fratl nodded.

Candal, Second Daughter, walked in.

Her mother handed her a filled cup and thought, finally she is home. Candal sat and took a sip. Then she looked at her mother.

"Ummmmmmm."

"House Mataraen was cross-tied with House Narkalar and House Energat. All those died. The family files indicate that House Mataraen has few other houses associated with it."

"Ah ummmm," said Anadaz. "I shall visit House Darthar Na."

Maine.

Early morning.

Ziaza walked from the sprawling cabin onto the porch and stretched. It had been a pleasant and very relaxing number of days. Much to her surprise she had found that she enjoyed sitting and talking with Ralph and Sandra. They were not like any of the stereotypes she had assumed them to be, given what they did for a living.

She set the coffee pot and cups on the table and watched the sun slowly flood the open space with early morning glow.

Sometime later, as Sandra finished preparing breakfast, refusing any help offered as she enjoyed doing that by herself, they heard the noise of a large pickup approaching, bringing a cloud of dust with it.

Sandra laughed. "Charles."

Ralph smiled and refilled his cup and Ziaza's.

Ziaza watched the truck and nodded. It was Charles. She looked at Sandra. "How did you know?"

Sandra set another place and began to serve as the truck parked at the other end of the cabin, sending the cloud of dust into the forest. "Charles does that all the time and no one can figure out how he does it."

"What?"

"Turn up just in time for a meal."

Charles slammed the door and strolled over to them, smiling. "Oh, boy! Breakfast!" And laughed, a loud happy sound.

"Morning" said Ziaza and began to eat. And thought to herself, that if you didn't know, Charles would just seem to be some large jock from some football team or other.

Charles dropped into the open chair, looked at the eggs on his plate, dosed them with hot sauce, and began to eat as well.

When they were done, Charles having made sure that there were no left-overs, Sandra brought out a new pot of coffee.

"What?" asked Ralph, looking at Charles. He could tell there was much to tell.

Charles grinned at him. "Soon you will rise from the dead." He winked at his friend. "Think we ought to wait until Easter?" And laughed.

"What?" restated Ralph.

So Charles explained. He told them what sort of papers he had been given by Swift and then told them of all the financial records that Sandra had given him, the records of The Flaming Sword of Truth Church Militant.

"And" prompted Ralph, knowing how Charles enjoyed being urged along during one of his complicated presentations.

Charles leaned forward, forearms on the table. "We have lots of documentation that links a certain corporate sleezeball and his hired henchman with that bunch of religious ding-bats and all the nasty stuff that came from that interaction. He used them and his henchman to do the dirty work."

"Oh," said Ralph.

"Randy's troops will pick them up," Charles looked at his wristwatch, "in fifteen minutes."

Ralph refilled their coffee cups and sighed. "Lots of turmoil and death just to build some sort of corporate money machine."

Charles nodded. "I would really like to do some very heavy thumping on those most responsible for that but most of them are dead." He grinned at Ziaza. "Vacation over?"

She stood. "Yes, it is." And smiled warmly at Sandra and Ralph. "Thanks." Ziaza handed the cell phone Charles had given her back to him.

Ralph smiled at Ziaza. "Feel free to use the cabin any time you need to get away and relax." He tossed her a spare key.

Sandra winked at her. "Bring a friend."

Ziaza winked back. "I'll just get my stuff and we can go."

As the truck hurtled down the road and away, Ralph helped Sandra clear the table. "Time for us to return as well."

"Wonder what interesting story Randy's troops have cooked up to explain our not-deaths?"

Ralph shrugged. "Ought to be quite interesting."

Washington, D.C.

They were crowded into F. Fred's office. He had one of the large offices so they were not all that crowded.

F. Fred filled the four glasses with a sparkling amber liquid and handed them around. "Sip it."

He dropped into his chair and looked from face to face as they sipped. J. Robert and the two Sallys, Anderson and Durtog.

"That Ralph Fredrickson is sneakier than anyone in this town." He set his glass on the desk and poured a little more into it. "And that says a whole lot."

"Well, Freddie," said Sally Anderson, "he certainly fooled everyone, including the ever snoopy media, and solved a big problem for us."

J. Robert nodded. "Franklyn and his hired goon are going away for a very long time. From what I hear, Franklyn's corporation was rather surprised at what he was up to."

S.A. took a small sip and wondered once again at the capacity of politicians to drink the way they do. "I wonder how Fredrickson could get so many government agencies to work together to pull this off. And how he could get his hands on all that material."

F. Fred looked at his empty glass and decided, *no*, and grumbled, "Anyone that can stroll as easily in and out of The White House as he does, can pull any string he feels like, it seems."

Maryland.

The six sat around the dining room table finishing their desert. It had been a rather ornate cake emblazoned in bright pink *And The Dead Shall Rise* in the center of the edible green-grass frosting with small edible grey tombstones artfully placed around the greeting.

Ralph refilled Sandra's wine glass and smiled at the others. "Good to be among the living again." He took a sip of the red wine that he was drinking. "Nice to be back from the woods as well. Shall we adjourn to the living room?"

Then he handed around a very large box of top of the line chocolates. "A gift from a boy Charles and I knew in grade school."

Charles winked at Randy.

And took a few.

House Darthar Na.

They were in one of the small comfortable rooms with a large outside window, Dee, Ternala, and Ar. On a small table sat a wooden box.

Dee nodded.

Ar stood and opened the box and took out a very ornate brooch and set it on the floor. Then he stepped back and said, "You are safe. Ternala, House Head awaits."

The brooch blurred and became a slim woman with decidedly blue skin. She stood slightly shorter than Ar.

"Andure, House Kaanatan skills trainer stands here. It is good to see Ternala Head alive." She bowed deeply.

Ternala brushed a tear from one cheek and smiled at her. "Welcome back. We have much work to do. House Antarax is doing much for us and we owe great debt to them."

The door opened and Jonathon walked in.

Dee nodded. "Do come visit, Ternala, when you have time."

Jonathon, Ternala, and Andure were gone.

Ar looked at Dee. "Princess, someone knocks. Winala answers."

Dee poured cups full and watched the door.

It opened and Winala walked in followed by a very tall woman who bowed deeply to Dee, straightened up, smiled warmly, and said, "Here is Anadaz, Head, House Ranadan, come to visit."

"Most welcome." Dee handed her and Winala a cup and sat. Ar left the room.

They sipped and looked out the window at the meadow and the forest.

"Ummmm," said Dee.

Anadaz took a sip and said, "I was visited by the Second Son of House Mataraen who stated that his house was greatly bothered by this house. This is what I learned about House Mataraen."

When she finished narrating, she held out her cup.

Dee refilled all the cups and took a sip from her's. "Would you like to visit The Fontala?"

"Most so," said Anadaz. "This one knows of our very long ago and the great vanishing of them."

Dee stood, setting her cup on a small table. "Shall we?"

"Lead on." Anadaz set her cup next to Dee's and stood.

Maine.

Doma Sparta wandered all around the destroyed compound and buildings, stepping carefully through all the debris, and then visited everyone who would tell him anything, even the most trivial, about the inhabitants of that place and anything else they knew.

Finished, he went to the closest hotel, took a room, and read and re-read everything he had written down, and stared at the few photographs.

Finally, over a very leisurely meal in the downstairs

restaurant as he dawdled over his dessert, it happened. He smiled at his dessert and to himself and admired what his mind could do when he wasn't trying to do anything.

Dark clothes! They had all dressed in dark clothes. So had been the one mentioned by his group's first one.

Over the previous three days he had spent his time once again wandering around the small town, talking with people here and there.

On the third day he bumped into a young man with a high curiosity who told him about following a large group that had snuck into the trees out there and who seemed to be watching that compound. So he had done the same thing.

Then he told Doma all that he had seen.

Doma shook his head in disbelief. And stopped as folk were staring at him. He stared across the table.

The young man had said that all were dressed in dark clothes, but the other things he told seemed to be wild and unreal, the product of an overactive imagination. Doma had smiled and said, yes, he believed what he was being told.

Some time later, after checking a license plate number that one person remembered, Doma drove toward Vermont.

House Darthar Na.

On the floor that was occupied by The Fontala, Dee led Anadaz to one of the smaller meeting rooms and introduced her to the First Hands of each of the seven stands. Then she introduced those who were called The One Who Remembers, the ones who held in their memories the past history of their stand.

Anadaz talked with them, asked probing questions, learned much, and then nodded. Her eyes scanned their faces and looked at Dee.

"It does seem to me that events very long ago and some not very long ago are linked to House Mataraen."

Then she explained what she meant by that.

Maryland.

It had been a busy number of days for them.

Now they were in Ralph's living room, after dinner, after dessert, each sitting in their favorite spot, sipping their favorite after dinner beverage.

Charles was grumbling.

Ralph had just told them that Franklyn had been given bail, a very large bail which he had paid, and was now under house arrest, complete with a fancy electronic bracelet and an order not to step outside the house. Franklyn had a very clever lawyer.

Ralph looked at Charles. "James James, he of the many names, is locked in a very secure cell with only himself for company."

Charles nodded. "Randy and I have guys back tracking, back tracing everything in all those documents."

"Ah," said Ralph. "So far, so good."

House Mataraen.

She rapped on the outside door and waited.

And waited.

And waited.

The door opened and he looked out.

"Yes?"

"Dee, Jonathon, Armilin, and Amadur, come to visit."

He stared at Armilin and Amadur. They wore jackets of a deep purple color and held long staffs in one hand. Armilin was wearing her silver chain mail under her jacket.

"Visit?"

"Just so," stated Dee.

Vermont.

She was relaxing on her back patio watching the birds jump around, switching from bird feeder to bird feeder.

She had just finishing talking with Jan, The Trail Runner sometime journalist, and had invited him over for dinner, telling him that he could come over earlier, if he wished. He said that he would be right there.

So she was relaxing, drinking tea, and wondering what sort of things Charles was now up to, especially after all that just past weirdness.

Her door bell rang.

"COME IN!"

She turned her head to watch him make his way out to the patio, frowned, and jumped to her feet.

"Who are you?" This guy was dressed all in brown colored, soft comfortable looking clothes. "What are you doing in my house? And what do you want?"

He smiled, a smile as soft as his garments.

"My name is Doma Sparta. You asked me in. I saw you and your group watching that walled place and running from there, as did I." He paused, eyes darting from bird feeder to bird feeder.

"May I sit and talk with you about that, about what you saw?"

Ziaza glared at him. "You a reporter?"

"No! Not at all."

She pointed at a chair. "O.K. Have some tea. And talk. I may not answer."

Doma sat, filled a glass, and tasted the beverage. "Quite

good. Thank you."

She dragged her chair around and sat facing him. "I am expecting a friend to visit. When he gets here, you are done."

Doma nodded, fished his journal from a side pocket of his jacket, opened it, and looked at her. "Let me read you what I saw. Tell me if I am wrong."

She nodded.

He began to read.

She halted him and snatched up the phone.

He watched and listened carefully.

Washington, D.C.

Charles sat at his desk sorting reports and stuffing them into one or another of the several folders on his desk. He had been doing this, off and on, for a number of days, mostly because it bored him to tears so he had stopped often and had worked on something else.

One of the many buttons on his phone began to flash. It was awhile before he noticed.

Sally Anderson sat at her desk reading her way through a rather lengthily piece of proposed legislation, scribbling notes on a pad of paper as she went.

Her door opened and Jons walked in, cleared her throat loudly, and dropped a newspaper on the desk.

"Read this."

The Congresswoman looked up and frowned at her number one assistant, picked up the newspaper, read a bit, and looked at her. "When did this happen?"

"Hot off the press."

Sally read the lengthily front page article, slowly. "Can we get more details?"

Jons shook her head. "Tried. No one will say anything beyond what is in that article. Franklyn is under house arrest, having paid a very large bail. His unnamed associate is in a jail somewhere."

Sally set the newspaper down. "Anything going to spill over onto us?"

Jons shook her head. "Don't think so. We were only in a first talking position and he went on his own way without us."

"Prepare a statement."

"I did."

"Coordinate with the others."

"I did."

Sally leaned forward and smiled. "I think that you need a raise in pay."

"Just doing my job."

"Better than most."

Jons smiled. "Franklyn will be the star of the coming media circus for quite some time."

Sally nodded. "Better him than us. Thanks."

Jons nodded and headed for her desk.

Sally began to read and scribble notes again.

Charles poked the button on his phone, having finally noticed it blinking.

"Ummmm?"

He jerked upright.

"WHAT?"

"Bring him to my office! . . . Just ask him! Uhhhhhh, just keep him there then!"

He nodded.

"O.K. Ahhh, thanks."

He punched another button, gave an order, punched a third button, and waited.

"Hi, Sandra. Can you and Ralph come to my office. Now! Ziaza is coming with a visitor and I think that we three need to talk to him."

He laughed. "Sure. Coffee and pastries."

He pushed one more button on the phone and gave that order.

House Antarax.

Zarpon and Ternala were strolling along a narrow path through the forest and finally walked out into a wide meadow. On the far side they could see a two story building and a great barn.

Zarpon pointed. "There stands the new House Kaanatan. In the barn they have built the birthing rooms." She smiled. "If needed."

They walked through the knee high grass and stopped in front of the stairs leading up to the front door.

The door opened and Andure, the house skills trainer, bowed deeply. "Welcome to House Kaanatan. Do come in."

Ternala laughed and hurried up the stairs tugging Zarpon along by one hand.

As they entered the house, Andure pointed out into the meadow. "Visitors." She hurried down the hall to gather up cups and coffee.

The visitors stopped at the base of the stairs and bowed.

"Here stands Karanly, First Sister, House Darthar, come to visit."

"Here stands Third Son, Canalon, House Qatan, come to visit."

"Here stands Second Daughter, Fairin, House Baldar,

come to visit."

"Here stands Second Daughter Dandal. Come to visit. House Tarkinal."

"Do come in," said Ternala. "All."

She led them down the hall and into the room Andure indicated and handed each of them a filled cup. The cups had been crafted by House Antarax.

Ternala took a sip, sat, waited, and after the proper amount of time, looked from face to face.

"Ummmmmmmmm."

Karanly smiled broadly. "Canalon, Fairin, and Dandal would join with House Kaanatan, ah umm, if the House Head does agree."

She stood and bowed to Ternala. And was gone.

Zarpon stood and bowed to Ternala. "The path that we followed is a shadow guarded trail, a house skill. None but Feyra can see it. We may visit back and forth." She turned and hurried from the room.

The discussion began.

Washington, D.C.

Charles leaned back in his chair as he sipped from the thick walled mug. On his desk sat a number of other similar mugs and a large carafe of coffee. Next to them sat a tray with a large assortment of pastries. He picked up one and began to munch upon it. It had been a few hours or so.

The door opened and they were ushered into the room by a young woman with a large gun holstered on her hip. She stood with her back to the door as she closed it and watched the pair as they sat in the chairs in front of Charles' desk.

Charles leaned forward and filled the two mugs.

"Coffee?"

And leaned back. "Take whatever you wish from the tray."

"Ziaza tells me," he said to the other, "that you have some interesting questions."

Doma nodded. Ziaza took a pastry.

A side door opened and Ralph entered the room carrying a cup. He took a sip and sat in a chair to one side and smiled. "Ziaza."

She smiled back and swallowed. "This is Doma Sparta. He belongs to an ancient order, an ancient group of people who have been trying to validate an ancient work by a man who claimed that he had seen a being with white wings dressed in dark clothes."

"Oh." Ralph took a sip.

Doma nodded. "I was one of the people observing that walled compound and ran for my life when all the, ah, excitement began."

"Someone," stated Ziaza, "wrote down my license plate number and he came to my house to visit. And ask questions." Ziaza refilled her cup. "He, ah, agreed to come here with me." She took another pastry from the tray. "Your driver was rather convincing." She smiled at Charles.

Charles leaned back. "O.K." He stared at Doma. "So, are we supposed to have white wings? We don't really dress in dark clothes and frighten far right crazies that believe in things like that!"

Doma pulled a thin volume from a patch pocket on his jacket and cleared his throat, opened it and read the first sentences.

"Once upon a time in the long ago past. It happened. A wise man saw an angel."

He looked from face to face. "My order has been

collecting bits and pieces of information, or tales, for several thousand years, searching for that reality. I do not believe in angels, or demons, or witches. That has been an error in belief and a waste of thousands of years." He emptied his cup. "May I?"

Charles nodded.

Doma refilled his cup and helped himself to one of the pastries.

"But, I am a very good observer. I believe, now, that there is a group of some kind, out there somewhere, who favor dark clothes, and who seem to have, ah, special skills." He jerked up his free hand to stop comments. And winced. "Ooop!" He had just scattered pastry crumbs across Charles' desk.

"I wished to ask this young woman some questions about what she saw to, ah, add to my observations. Now, here we are." He stuffed the remainder of the pastry in his mouth, chewed, and waggled the free hand. "Where ever here might be."

Charles looked at Ralph.

Ralph nodded, pulled out his cell phone, and touched a button. "Hello. Come to Charles' office."

Moments later came a knock on the door. The guard stepped aside and opened it. Sandra walked in.

"Dear?"

"This is Doma Sparta. Ziaza brought him here, in a manner of speaking. He is searching for some, ah, group that tends to dress in dark garb and apparently have, ummm, special skills. His, ahhhh, order has been searching for thousands of years because their, ah, founder, umm, saw an angel with white wings."

Sandra pulled a chair next to Ralph and sat. He handed

her his cup.

"I am not sure what we ought to do." Ralph leaned forward. "About white wings and dark clothes."

Ziaza stared at them and then at Charles.

"Charles, I think that there is a whole lot I don't know but that I think I ought to know." She set her mug on his desk. "Or is this one of those you don't need to know things."

Charles looked over at Ralph and then at Sandra.

Sandra stood. "I'll be right back." She walked through the side door and closed it.

Shortly thereafter she walked back into the room and shook her head. "Not home. Some sort of complicated piece of business that requires resolution."

Ralph looked at Charles.

Charles smiled. "Well, Doma, looks like you are going to be our guest for a little while."

Doma gasped. "Am I arrested?"

"Not exactly."

Ziaza jumped to her feet. "Charles?"

"Perfectly safe. Just a sticky problem to solve." He shrugged. "Might take a few days." He looked at Ralph.

"Let's hope not," said Ralph.

House Mataraen.

They were ushered into a room with a table set with a number of chairs, steaming cups sitting in front of each chair.

A large robust male rose from his chair and looked from face to face.

"Here is Zarten, Head, House Mataraen!"

They bowed deeply and waited until he sat before they did.

They sipped and waited.

"Ummmmmmm," said Zarten.

Dee nodded and took a sip.

"Here is Daliera Fontala, Head of House Darthar Na."

She gestured to one side.

"Here sits Othara, Head of House Darthar."

She gestured to the other side.

"Here sits Armilin, House Induna, The One of the All of The Fontala. Here sits Armadur, First Hand, First Stand, of The Fontala."

"Ah ummmm."

Dee nodded and took a sip.

"Word has come that House Mataraen is bothered by some, ah ummmm, activities of House Darthar Na."

"Just so," grumbled Zarten. "Just so!"

Dee set her cup on the tale and pushed it forward.

"This one feels that some reflection on our very long ago is pertinent."

"Ummmmmm."

"House Head Zarten must remember from very long ago the occurrence called The Great Straightening. House Darthar was very long ago, and does so remain, The Bringer of Order, the one that made The Feyra as they are very long ago and now."

Zarten nodded and looked from Dee to Jonathon and back again.

"And," continued Dee, "in the very long ago, during that, ah, straightening, House Darthar Na came into existence, then known, and now known, as The Protectors of the Innocent, and the home of The Fontala."

She took a sip and stared into Zarten's eyes.

"I am The Word of The Fontala, their head. Armilin is my voice to The Fontala, The Second in Standing. I am Daliera, the second one so named. I am Daliera who woke The Fontala from their long sleep, who brought them back from their very long ago lost time, to once again be The Protectors of the Innocent."

She set her cup down, slowly stood and pointed at Zarten.

"I am greatly bothered by House Mataraen, a shadow house who was much involved by those few in the very long ago and the not very long ago who think to tell all The Feyra how they must live, and behave, and think! We are few and widely scattered and do not require such!"

She leaned forward, both hands flat on the table top. "How say you, Zarten?"

He took a sip and watched her sit.

"Word says that House Darthar Na has one of the people as a frequent visitor. A thing never done by the Feyra."

"Just so." She picked up her cup and took a sip.

"The Feyra have avoided such since the very long ago."

"Just so."

He cleared his throat and rasped, "Why?"

"The people helped me find and rescue survivors of House Kaanatan, almost totally destroyed and eliminated by a small cluster of very not nice people. Without their aid, House Kaanatan would be no more."

He jerked back in his chair. "Never has such been done!"

"Just so." She nodded. "The people, unknowingly, helped me find The Shadow Feyra, very long ago hidden from us. I provided a home for them among us."

He stared at her. "They exist?"

"Just so."

Dee took a sip and indicated Armilin with her free hand.

"House Induna kept, preserved, and passed on the staff

skills of The Fontala long ago after their disappearance from Feyra understanding. House Induna did this, only House Induna!"

Dee glared at him and banged her cup on the table. "It is House Mataraen that bothers the fabric of The Feyra. It is House Mataraen that caused the long sleep and the almost loss of The Fontala."

She snatched up her cup, stood and held it out toward him. "House Mataraen has great debt to all The Feyra, for that. House Mataraen owes great debt for the ending of Houses Nagaron and the Seventh Stand of The Feyra. House Mataraen owes great debt for the ending of House Energat. House Mataraen owes great debt for the almost ending of House Narkalar!"

Zarten leaped to his feet and batted the cup from her hand. "Impertinence!"

Dee thrust her hand, palm outward, at him. Zarten hurtled backward, knocking over his chair, thudding into the far wall. "That was a non-lethal house skill."

She watched him heave himself to his feet.

"Do nothing," she growled, "if you value House Mataraen, else very lethal skills are shown!"

The door banged open as house members crowded into the room. Armilin and Amadur whirled around and jumped to either side, long staves glowing soft purple light.

Jonathon slowly stood and threw his cup.

It bounced off Zarten's forehead.

"Think carefully, Zarten!" he ordered. "House Mataraen has been outside The Feyra Order since very long ago. During The Great Straightening, clusters and houses who thought this way, became no more. Is that the obligation the House Head has to House? To be no more?"

He turned and looked at the house members. "Is it?"

A large robust male stepped forward and bowed to Jonathon.

"Here is First Son, Ndana, Anointed One. No, it is not the obligation of House Head to House. Since the very long ago House Mataraen has followed a path of believing much of self and little of The Feyra. Some do not learn. During The Great Straightening, The Dark Nine Cluster, and, ah umm, others during the very long ago have urged and caused great loss, doing very not nice." He bowed deeply to Dee and Jonathon.

Straightening up, he pointed at Zarten. "I am The Anointed One, now House Head!" He shook his head. "House Mataraen will no longer be a shadow house. No longer a house to tell others what to do. No more, no more."

Zarten stared at him. "NEVER!"

"So be it," stated Jonathon, pointing at Zarten.

Dust settled to the floor.

Ndana looked at Jonathon. "Name the debt."

"None."

Jonathon stepped close to Dee and beckoned Armilin and Amadur to stand near.

"Home," said Dee.

Washington, D.C.

A gentle knock and the door swung open.

Sally looked up as her number one assistant walked in clutching a thick stack of newspapers in her arms.

"Jons?"

The papers thudded on top of the desk.

"Big news, big, big news, in every type of print media," stated Jons.

"What?"

"Franklyn. I read the first one and bought copies of everything. You, F. Fred, etc., are mentioned very deep in these articles. Not a whole lot, but mentioned as associates of that sleeze."

Sally sighed and picked up the top newspaper and began to read. Finished, she sighed. "Might have known."

Jons handed her several sheets. "Here's our statement, direct and to the point, no dodging around at all. I phoned the others and talked with them. Everyone is following your lead." She smiled.

Sally stood. "Let's go to lunch. Somewhere expensive. I want to smile and look unconcerned for the media hounds." She laughed. "And have a really good lunch. You deserve it."

They left her office, arm in arm.

House Darthar Na.

Dee was relaxing in one of the small comfortable rooms with a large outside window, sipping coffee and looking at forest and meadow.

Jonathon had gone home. Armilin and Amadur had walked upstairs to hold a meeting of all The Fontala so all would know what had transpired at House Mataraen.

Dee had sent her daughter, Tiela, to visit House Ranadan so they would be informed as well.

So, she was relaxing and writing the end of the novel she had been working on. If Janice didn't turn up soon she would need to travel to The Wild Garden and see what was going on.

Someone knocked on the door and walked in.

"Sandra? What?" Sandra was frowning.

"We have a problem and really have no idea what to do about it."

"Ummmmmm."

"Can you come? To Charles' office?"

Dee stood and nodded. And wondered what strange thing the people were up to now.

Washington, D.C.

Sandra and Dee walked in from the adjoining room.

Charles, Ziaza, and Doma watched them enter. Ralph nodded and took a bite from the pastry that he held.

Charles filled a cup from an insulated jug and handed it to Dee who sat in a chair facing the others, and took a sip.

Sandra opened a cabinet, removed a glass, filled it with amber liquid, took a sip, and then sat in a corner to watch them all.

Charles indicated the man. "This is Doma Sparta. He can explain who he is, what he is doing, and all that."

Dee nodded and took a sip.

Doma smiled at her, opened the thin book he held and read the first page. Then he began to explain, everything that he had seen, everything that he knew, and everything that he now thought.

When he finished, Dee nodded and held out her cup. Charles filled it.

"So, Doma," said Dee, "what do you think?"

He smiled at her. "You dress in dark clothes."

"Just so. Many do."

"Indeed."

"Your, ah umm, group dress in brown."

"Indeed."

"So?"

Doma cleared his throat.

"What do I think? Good question." He sipped at his

coffee.

"I think that there exists those of whom we know nothing. We have been searching for a few thousand years and have learned nothing, really nothing at all. But!" He held up one finger. "They are out there. Out there somewhere. I was hoping that Ms. Ziaza could tell me what she did see. But instead, I am here. Interesting."

"Not very," grumbled Charles. "Ziaza, who works, in a manner of speaking, sometimes, for us, is a very skilled observer, nothing else. She doesn't need to be bothered. By anyone."

Doma nodded, his eyes carefully studying Dee's face. "Tell me, Miss, have you ever seen a being with white wings? Or dark wings?"

Dee smiled at him. "Creatures of mythology."

"Who wear dark clothing," added Doma.

"If you wish." She took a sip.

"You like coffee?"

"Just so." She took a sip.

"May I leave?"

Dee looked at Charles who pushed a button and said something softly into the phone.

"Done," he said to Doma. "A car and driver will take you back to your vehicle."

The door swung open and a man walked in. "This way, Mr. Sparta." And led him from the room and down the hall, closing the door behind them.

Ziaza glared at Charles and then at Dee.

"So, who are you really, Dee Grant?"

"Just an author." She shrugged.

Ziaza jabbed a finger at Charles and frowned. "Humbug!"

"A friend." Dee smiled. "So are Ralph and Sandra."

Ziaza sighed. "Secrets inside of secrets inside of secrets."

Charles' phone flashed a bright green button. He pushed it as he picked up the phone. "Yes?" Then he laughed. "Bring him." And hung up.

Charles leaned back and beamed at Ziaza.

"What?" she snapped.

"There is a very agitated young man about to arrive. It seems he saw you and Doma being driven away, followed that car, and is just now in our lobby demanding to know what we were doing to, or, with you."

The door opened and he hurried in past the woman with him. Her gun seemed to jump into her hand.

"Jan!" gasped Ziaza.

Charles waggled his hand and the woman left closing the door. He looked up at Jan. "What did you think you were doing? Jan?"

He stared at them. "D. Grant?"

Dee nodded. "Just so."

Jan dropped into the chair where Doma had sat. "Boy, am I ever confused."

Charles poked a button, spoke softly, and hung up.

"Take him away, Ziaza." He opened his desk, took out a slip of paper and handed it to her.

"The driver will take you to a nice restaurant and wait while you two have a leisurely meal."

The door opened and a woman looked in. "Car's ready."

After they were gone, Charles slid a folder from inside his desk, slipped out a single sheet of paper, and handed it to Dee. "Your copy. Now we know what happened to Sandrel's parents and why."

Dee took the sheet and stood.

"Home?" asked Sandra.

Dee followed her into the adjoining room.

Charles locked his desk and did the same thing. He went home as soon as Ralph left.

Into The Woods. Or Something Like That.

Dee and Sandra looked at it. It was a hole. In a cliff. High on a mountain side. They had come here following Dee's directions.

The cliff stretched dark grey and light grey bands far to either side. There was only the one hole. Here and there, crooked and warped vegetation clung to small crevices making small green spots on all those grey tones.

Dee pointed at the tunnel. "Stay out here, Sandra. It will be safe."

She walked deep inside the tunnel. This was something that she didn't want Sandra to know about. Then they would go home.

The walls glowed dull green light. She turned a bend and stopped. At the door in the wall. And knocked.

"Kakmir!" growled something, somewhere. That told Dee that the one she wanted to visit was at home.

She thumped on the door. "Open! Dee, come to visit!"

"Do dak gar pit zik! Piz zik!"

"SILENCE!" roared someone as the door creaked inward. A short, rather globular figure stood there, peering out, all of four feet tall, wearing a bright yellow something or other, appearing most like a tent turned into a garment.

"Ah hum. Do come in." The speaker backed up, and turned, speaking to her as he wobbled down the tunnel. "Don't mind the door thing. Still in training. I remember you."

"Strange, strange, strange, strange," mumbled Dee to

herself as she followed him, or it, or whatever. It was just as she remembered when she had visited here before with Jonathon.

Her host dropped into a chair set next to a table and waggled an appendage at the other chairs. As soon as she sat, a mug was shoved at her.

She picked up her mug and took the tiniest of sips. And held the liquid in one cheek. She knew better than drink it. The last visit here was a disaster. For her stomach.

Hondo took a great swallow. "GOOD! GOOD! DRINK!"

The stuff was awful, gut wrenching horrible.

"You are still one of the several that rents things?"

"We try harder!" Hondo banged his mug on the table. Dee took a tiny sip and added it to the little already held in her cheek. He refilled his mug and eyed her's.

Then she told Hondo what she wished, and why, and asked if he could do that.

Hondo nodded. "Very not nice folk!"

She nodded. "This has to be a secret."

"SECRET!" bellowed Hondo. "Big, dark secret."

She handed him a sheet of paper and then another with carefully written instructions on it.

"Great debt is owed."

"A deal!" Hondo settled somewhat lower in his chair. "But no tell, ever."

"Absolutely," agreed Dee.

Dee stood, and bowed. She hurried from the room and down the long hall, tunnel, and outside.

She walked quickly to the nearby meadow, spun away and decorated a handy shrub with Hondo's drink. "Horrible. Ghastly."

"Take me home, Sandra."

The Free Floating Mind.

Dee and Janice had been on a book tour, for a number of months, wandering across the United States from large book store to large book store. It was the standard route, established some time ago by Janice and agreed to by Dee's publisher. Janice carried a company credit card and a zippered small case stuffed with expense money. The case of money had been agreed to by Dee's publisher at Dee's insistence and after much grumbling by the head man who had stared at her and wondered why all authors were that way, beyond understanding.

Now Dee and Janice were at the end of the big store tour. This was the last stop.

She sat on the small platform on the hard chair, the hard-backed folding chair and watched the people settling down in the rows of similar marginally comfortable folding chairs. She took a sip from the tall paper cup with the paper insulating sleeve slipped around it. And waited.

A tall somewhat slender man, dressed in a pastel pink colored shirt and trousers stepped up to the small podium and cleared his throat.

"Welcome," he began, and waited for them to quiet down. "Welcome to the Free Floating Mind Bookstore and tonight's event. Our guest author is one you all know and have read and enjoyed. Tonight she will answer questions first and then she will read the first two chapters of her newest novel which continues the on-going saga of those new and unusual characters that came into existence in that new fantasy genre all her own. As it stated on the dust jacket, she wrote this while she was on an extended vacation, meeting new people and finding new inspiration."

He laughed. "But here she is, back and well-rested, and

ready to read and discuss the third volume. Please warmly welcome tonight's guest, D. Grant!"

In the midst of the applause, she stepped up to the small podium, shook his hand, and took a sip from her cup, and waited.

Finally she held out her free hand, and smiled at them. "Questions? Before I read?"

Hands shot up.

She pointed at a young woman.

"Miss Grant, why are you the damsel in distress in your new book?"

Dee laughed. "All my other books have had one so I thought it might be fun, and interesting, to be one in my own story." She sipped. "After all, it is more interesting to see my book from the inside out, so to speak."

A man waved his hand. "Aren't your main characters rather hard on the vampire literature as it is being written today? Or yesterday?"

Dee nodded. "I suppose." She grinned. "But then, that is just the way that they see things." She winked at the questioner.

And so it went until she halted them so she could start the last part of the evening's presentation. She thought to herself, it really was fun being an author.

She took a sip, cleared her throat, and began to read.

"Chapter One . . . "

People sat back and relaxed into the story.

Virginia.

The large pickup parked behind one of the many police cars that crowded along the curb in front of the large and sprawling house in an area of large and sprawling and very expensive houses. In the driveway an ambulance was backed up with the rear doors swung wide. Uniformed police stood in small clusters here and there as well as others dressed in suits.

Charles jumped from the driver's seat and waited until Ralph walked around to join him.

"Let's go around to the back," suggested Charles, leading Ralph past the three-car garage and down the paved walkway to the back gate.

The strolled over the patio and up to where the back door opening into the kitchen had been. Standing back, staring into the kitchen they could see a number of investigators slowly crawling amidst the debris picking up this or that piece and sealing them in evidence bags.

One of them looked up. "You'll have go around and come in the front door."

"What happened here?" asked Charles.

The man shrugged. "Something blew the kitchen door, door jamb, and sections of the attached wall into and through the kitchen and partway down the hall. So far we haven't found any trace of explosive, or anything else, to explain what did it." He went back to work.

Charles shrugged and headed back to the front of the building, Ralph walking at his side.

They stopped at the front door and signed the clipboard held by the policewoman manning the door and controlling the flow of personnel in and out of the crime scene.

She glanced down to see who these guys were. Then she stared at Ralph. "The White House?"

He nodded and smiled at her as they stepped past.

She pointed, told them to go down the hall, and up the stairs to where they should be able to hear the voices.

As they walked across the living room, they heard her

mumble, "Damn politicians are gonna make this into a political mess."

At the top of the stairs they headed down the long hall toward the conversation coming from an open door.

They stopped and peered inside.

The large man in the rumpled suit turned and stared at them. "I am Detective Ransom. Who are you and stay out of here!"

Charles flipped open a thin leather case as did Ralph.

Ransom stepped close enough to read. "And why are you here?"

Ralph smiled. "We are the ones responsible for the arrest of Franklyn and associate for a number of crimes. Where is he?"

The Detective laughed, a hollow sound. "Step just inside the door, no further."

As they did they could see blood on the floor, on the walls, and splattered across the ceiling.

Both looked around the room for the body.

Charles frowned.

Ralph looked at Detective Ransom.

The Detective waved one hand at the room.

"Where is Franklyn? Everywhere, he is everywhere."

"What happened? Here?" Ralph's eyes searched the room for the body or body parts.

Ransom shrugged. "Haven't the foggiest idea. Never saw anything like this before." He stepped closer to them. "You guys have any ideas you want to share?"

"Nope," said Charles. "We just wanted to see what had happened to our bad guy."

Ransom stared at Ralph. "You taking over the case? You can have it, if you want it. I will be glad to get rid of it."

"No." Ralph shook his head. "Let's go, Charles." He nodded at Ransom. "Best of luck."

Ransom laughed as they headed back down the hall.

They were driving down the main road, the one they had come by, when Ralph reached over and poked Charles on the shoulder.

"What is going on?"

"As Detective Ransom said, no idea."

"And?" prompted Ralph.

"James James is also kaput."

"What?"

"He was found dead in his cell. Unlike Franklyn, he was all in one piece, just dead."

"And?"

"No idea. He was in a cell, deep inside the establishment all by himself. We had some of our guys monitoring the situation and anyone who was allowed to approach the cell. No one saw anything. He went to sleep and when morning came he was dead. No trace of poison, no wounds, no nothing. Coroner is going to have a major problem on his hands because a number of folk are going to want to know what happened."

He glanced at Ralph and back to the road.

"What?"

"His face was frozen in an expression of fright, or terror, something like that."

"Oh."

"Yep," said Charles.

Just Another Small Town.

This was their last stop after wandering the United States for a number of months, popping into a number of the larger urban areas, visiting the bookstores. It was a book tour for her new book, just as she had promised her publisher. The pair of them, the author and her tour organizer, had gotten, again, some small amount of tired from answering the same old questions, asked over and over and over again. It was interesting in a strange sort of a way. But tiring. As it always was.

She had suggested to Janice, once again, that maybe they could just create a handout with those same questions and the usual answers printed on it. That way, she hoped, someone would ask something new. Her companion had argued that it wasn't a good idea and she had agreed. Once again.

Finally, they were visiting some of the small towns and their bookstores, often the only bookstore, and giving the stores and whoever might be there more of an unprepared show and tell than the usual thing that they did. It was fun to be spontaneous and relaxed rather than programmed.

Now, here they were, two females, Dee and Janice, in a small town in one of the western states, well off the main road, having a meal in the only restaurant. This small town was becoming one of their favorite places to visit.

"Still much better than the usual hotel restaurant stuff." She licked the frosting off her lips and smiled at her traveling companion. "Much better."

Janice nodded. "I agree. Here we are again, out here in the middle of nowhere again. In this town again. You are not going to shove that large guy through a window again, are you? Not after they apologized on our last visit and treated us to beer and pretzels." She laughed.

Dee smiled. "No, he is safe. All those big urban book stores look alike. Out here I can see open spaces, talk with a few people at a time, listen to the quiet, and begin to think, ummm ah, about my new novel." She laughed. "So when you call the publisher again, you can tell him that. It will make him happy."

She waved at the only waitress, who strolled over, and looked down at her. "Somethin?"

"Yes. I would like another piece of that pie. And more coffee, please." She looked across the table.

"Just coffee, please."

The waitress shuffled over to the pie case, a circular pie container with a number of shelves inside a clear plastic shell, cut a chunk from the appropriate pie, slid it onto a plate, and returned, and set it on the table.

"Here ya go, Dearie. Coffee is just finished. I'll bring you a pot." She winked. "I do enjoy seeing someone who enjoys what we fix. I remember you. Welcome back." She wandered away, came back, refilled their coffee cups, and headed into the back to talk with the cook. And make a few phone calls.

Dee smiled and cut a big chunk off the slice with her fork. "Nice country. Lots of open space and mountains. And good dessert."

"When you are done, let's just take another stroll around for awhile. We can cruise the main drag, such as it is. See if anything has changed. See how your number one fans are doing." Janice laughed.

"Sure."

"Ahhhh, Dee."

"What?"

"My father just send a call. He said that one of his regular customers asked him if he ever heard of a collector named Doma Sparta. Mr. Sparta wanted to place an open order for anything dealing with folk wearing dark clothes and having white wings. My father told that dealer that the request sounded rather peculiar but that at the moment he didn't think he had anything on the shelves that would fit such a request."

"Ah ummmmmm." Dee finished her dessert and sipped at her coffee.

As soon as they were finished, they paid the bill, left a generous tip, and walked outside.

Janice pointed. "As I remember, the edge of town is over there."

They strolled that way in the gathering dusk. And as they wandered down the sidewalk the sky darkened and the few street lights came on. They heard no traffic or any other sounds. It was still a very quiet town.

"Still quite a small place," said Dee. They had hit the edge of town. So they turned and wandered back toward the other edge of town. As they walked along she wondered what she ought to do about Doma.

"Certainly is," agreed Janice. "With one not too bad motel, one pretty good restaurant, the one and only bar in town with a rather unkempt exterior and a brand new large window, still washed and clean, and that little bookstore is still in business."

They walked over to the bookstore and reintroduced themselves to the owner and the few customers.

Then they talked, the author and the few customers, about the usual things. Dee smiled to see that her books were still on display. "Thanks," she said to the owner.

Then they walked in. Two very large men, who stopped, and stared at them. One mouth dropped open. Both men were wearing heavy, badly worn work boots, dirty denim jeans and denim jackets over faded shirts of some barely visible pattern. Both stomachs were threatening of overflow wide leather belts.

One stepped up to Dee and looked down at her.

"My, my, my," he said.

"Good to see you again," said the other. "Right, Little Fred?"

Little held out a well thumbed book. "Ahhhh, Ms. Grant, would you sign my book? It is your most recent one."

Rance did the same thing with the book that he held as Little stepped back. The pair had heard that Dee and her friend were in the bookstore. It was a small town and the waitress liked to talk on the phone.

Dee laughed. "I would be most happy to do so, gentlemen."

The book store owner stared at her. No one ever dared to call Rance and Little Fred gentlemen, not to their faces. Then she remembered that Dee had said the same thing to them the last time she had visited. It was something to wonder about.

Dee signed their books. "So, may we buy both of you a beer or two or three?"

Rance held out his arm. She slipped her arm around his. It was a very large arm.

"Come into my parlor," laughed Rance, "and we will just do that. We have a special table in there now. We named it, The Author's Corner." He laughed, a booming laugh that rattled the small window of the bookstore. "Come on, Little. Let's go drink a bunch of beer. And show off our favorite author. I think there are probably a few other fans waiting, wanting their books signed as well."

New Mexico.

On top of a high hill two figures stood and looked out over and across the wide valley, all greys and browns. They hadn't been there a moment ago.

Down below, out on the flats, adjacent to a, more or less,

single lane dirt road sat a cluster of buildings that surrounded a large patio.

Their eyes scanned here and there but there was little to see. There was no traffic on that road. The settlement appeared to be quiet. They didn't see anyone moving about.

They waited. And saw a man walk from one of the buildings and stroll along a narrow path and out into all that desolation.

Doma Sparta had walked along this game trail many times before. The local wildlife had made the game trail in their journey from one side of the wide valley to the other side. While they used it to travel from one place to another he used it to think. He had found that when he was on one of his long walks that he was actually engaged in a kind of moving meditation. At those times he was totally unaware of his surrounding environment. But during the day it was perfectly safe. Those who had created the path only utilized it at night.

"Hello, Doma."

He took three steps before the voice registered. Jerking to a halt, Doma stopped and turned to see who had spoken to him.

"You!" He frowned. "Are you really there?"

Dee smiled at him. "Just so."

He took two steps closer to her and stopped.

"I didn't hear any vehicle traffic. This road is rarely traveled by anyone." How could she be here?

She shook her head. "No car."

"I don't understand." He looked around, checking the great emptiness, walked over, and sat on one of the large boulders that were widely scattered in this area. And stared at her.

She walked over and sat on another boulder that was

close by.

"Curiosity," she said.

"Curiosity? About what?"

"Your, ah, group has been seeking confirmation of your originator's vision, is that not so?"

He nodded. "Yes. But it was not a vision, at least we do not believe that it was. As I stated in Charles' office, we believe that there are others," he waggled one arm, "out there. That is what he saw, one of them."

She nodded. "What will your group do, after spending all that time and effort, if you finally find something that says that what he saw was, or is, so?"

Doma smiled. "A good question. It deals with purpose and existence." He nodded. "A good question." And stared at her. "A good question never asked by anyone." He shrugged. "I fear my comrades, and I, have allowed the search to become the end all and be all of our existence."

"So it is an endeavor without end?"

Doma sighed. "Let us suppose that we find someone, wings and all. What does that mean? To us? To our existence? Is that the question, ah, questions?"

Dee nodded. "Just so." She set down the small pack, opened it, removed a thermos and two cups, and filled them. She handed him one and took a sip from the other.

He took a sip. "Coffee. Quite good."

She took a sip and waited.

"I have no idea." He took a sip. "What would we do? Then? To finally find what one seeks could be very frightening to many. History is littered with folk who did and were rejected by their own for killing their purpose in life." He sighed. And took a sip and stared at the ground for a long time.

He looked up, tears running down his cheeks. "Tell me,

please? Does what I believe to be true to be actual reality, or merely the figment of a long ago person's imagination? Is it true? Do you know?"

"What will you do, Doma, if that is true? What he saw." She watched his face carefully.

His shoulders slumped. "What else can I do? I know how to search? I know how to write about what I find. I have no other skills. But to search for what is already known is pointless." He sighed.

"Soooooo?"

He held out his cup. She refilled it.

Doma straightened up. "I suppose that I would have to find something else to do. Something similar, something else to search for. Something else to study and understand, to write about."

"And your fellows, what will they do?"

"Ahhhhh, yes." He shook his head. "I do not think that they actually want to know. I think that if I found that which we seek that I couldn't tell them. History is also filled with those who speak that to folk who refuse to acknowledge such and are often killed." He took a sip. "I enjoy life too much to do something to end it that way."

"Would you be willing to write a history that spans more than the existence of your, ah ummmm, order. Writing down and organizing many oral histories that are all linked into one large total history."

"Intriguing."

"You would have to travel to do that. You would have to be the only one. It would take the rest of your life to do."

Doma smiled and took a sip.

"Are you offering me a chore because my own is over?"

Dee stood and refilled his cup. "Yes."

He looked up and nodded. "Yes. I would do that." And smiled at her.

"One never to be shared by any of your group?"

He nodded

"You are sure that you could do something like that?"

He nodded.

Dee pointed. "Look there."

Doma looked and squinted his eyes. "I see someone way over there, a mere speck on top of that tall hill."

"If you run, you will die."

"What?"

"Your first one saw the first head of my house."

Doma jumped to his feet and gasped.

Her great feather covered wings slowly waggled white in the sunlight.

He dropped onto his rock. "Chemicals in my coffee! You put something in my coffee!"

"We do not do that, Doma Sparta!" She lifted up. "What do you see, Searcher?"

He gasped for air. "A being with white wings dressed in dark clothes."

She settled in front of him. "I am not anything in your mythology." The wings disappeared.

He slowly nodded.

"Sooooooo, Doma, what would you do?"

"A written history of white wings and dark clothes?"

Dee smiled. "Ever so much more." She pointed. Something lifted into the air from that distant hill and soared on great wings toward them.

"You are about to start. You have ever so much to do and to see. We need a written history."

House Darthar Na.

The room looked like the throne rooms seen in every costume drama set in the era of knights that Hollywood had ever made. The ceiling was arched, the walls all ornate wood paneling. Opposite the door, next to the far wall was a raised platform upon which sat the throne. It was a rather plain wooden chair with a cushion seat and a high padded back and arm rests.

She walked down the central path, lighter stone than the rest of the floor, past the clusters of those standing, waiting, up the steps and sat down, and smiled. She did feel rather regal sitting up here looking down at those gathered here. She smiled and thought, all this place needs is lots of folk standing around in fancy clothes and large guards dressed in heavy armor holding great swords. But those now gathered here weren't even a little like that.

She leaned back in the chair. It was quite comfortable.

Ar stood by her right side.

Jonathon and Karanly stood on the floor toward her right side, not too close, not too far away.

On her left there was a cluster of individuals who were being stared at by the bulk of those in the room.

Ar leaned close and whispered in her ear. She nodded. And beckoned Jonathon and Karanly to step close.

Dee sat straighter, eyes searching the many faces.

"I am going to introduce all, beginning with myself."

She stood and bowed deeply to them all. "I am Daliera Fontala. We, The Feyra, do not name ourselves in this manner, tagging on a family name. My name is a contraction of the name some have called me, Daliera of The Fontala. It tells that I am Daliera, Head of House Darthar Na, and that I am Daliera of The Fontala as well."

Her hand indicated a group that stood there wearing jackets of a deep purple color and holding a long staff vertically by their left side.

"There is Armilin. The One of The All, of The Fontala. House Induna. The one who speaks for me to The Fontala."

She nodded and indicated a pair.

"Amadur, First Hand, First Stand, House Argonar. Farlon, The One Who Remembers, House Faradon."

Then she indicated the next grouping and named each pair in succession.

"Meludo, First Hand, Second Stand, House Telat. Delat, The One Who Remembers, House Trillmar. Cantala, First Hand, Third Stand, House Zbtan. Trakatar, The One Who Remembers, House Nerian. Stregt, Fourth Stand, First Hand, House Ovever. Wisuot, The One Who Remembers, House Zilan. Mensta, First Hand, Fifth Stand, House Darunat. Udoat, The One Who Remembers, House Hantaz. Oatut, First Hand, Sixth Stand, House Quartep-Vierda. Uztal, The One Who Remembers, House Abalam. Kitea, First Hand, Seventh Stand, House Induna, Anagon, The One Who Remembers, House Naztan. Yallan, The Seeker, House Farback."

She bowed to them. "These are those who listen and direct The Fontala, long asleep but now once again with us, The Feyra."

She sat and smiled at a small group. "These are the Heads of the Darthar Sub-Houses. Suta Namel, suta Ean, suta Zbtan, suta Dundar, suta Milaton who gifted the *Hamel*, the Ice Cats to my daughters, suta Ocedaron, and suta Farbin."

She indicated the next group and smiled. "My Cousin-Houses. Dalir, Head Parlente. Namata, Head Fam. Induna, Head Armilin, Anointed One, and The One of The All as I mentioned. Patal, a deeply hidden Cousin House, whose Head wished to remain hidden and who gave the Word's Ring back to me when all thought that it had been lost in the very long ago in the spot where the Seventh Stand perished. Angorson, Head Pardosh. Anathor, Head Fraz."

She stood and bowed to each of the groups. Then she turned and bowed deeply. "Here stands Othara, Head of House Darthar and Lord of the Darthar Family, Karanalador, First Sister, House Darthar, and Damadon to my daughters."

She turned slightly and beckoned them forward. "Here stands House Sextet, an adopted House to House Darthar Na. Ralph Fredrickson, Head, his mate, Sandra, and Sandrel, adopted daughter, The Anointed One."

The trio bowed deeply to the gathering.

"Ralph and Sandra," explained Dee, "are of The People. Sandrel is Feyra, House Kaanatan."

Dee turned her head and waved him forward. He stepped carefully to the front accompanied by another and turned to look out at everyone. "Here stands Doma Sparta of The People, once a member of a small group of the people who called themselves The Searchers, now The Historian of The Feyra, and Hakar, Third Brother, House Darthar." She bowed to them.

Then she sat and leaned back and waited for the murmuring to die away. And pointed

"These people are special. Sandra, House Sextet, whose sister raised Sandrel after some very not nice ones of The People almost eliminated House Kaanatan, learned a House Darthar skill because I asked her to try and do that. All of House Sextet are friends and helped preserve House Kaanatan and were responsible, unwittingly, in our locating The Shadow Feyra and giving them a home in House Darthar Na, a fact few Feyra know."

She smiled at all the puzzled and worried looking faces. "Almost never have The Feyra interacted with The People for good and ancient reasons, although there have been a few known cases where it had been done. But, I have interacted, as have The Fontala, and The Feyra have benefitted. Later, over food and coffee I will tell in detail all any wish to know."

She pointed. "I asked Doma to begin to write down our history, The History of The Feyra. Hakar will aid him in this endeavor. In the very long ago, The Seventh Stand of The Fontala perished. When they did, one seventh of the history of The Fontala perished as well. Now, in the house library, we have the written history of The Fontala. The Ones Who Remember have been very busy seeing that this is so. What was only oral history cannot be lost, ever again."

She stood. "Perhaps because I was given people memories I feel this should not be so. I believe our total history if too valuable to lose!"

She set her hand on Ar's shoulder. "Ar, House Darthar Na skills trainer is having copies made of all the volumes of The Fontala history. These will be sent to our large libraries so all Feyra may read and know."

She smiled at them. "Our lives are long as are our memories. All of our history should survive so all The Feyra may know it, if they wish. I called all here to say this and know how strange this must seem. We will meet with all in two people days. The decision is your's. The question to be answered is this! Should we write our history so that it is never to be lost?"

She bowed even more deeply to them and then strolled from the room accompanied by Jonathon, Karanly, House Sextet, and Doma and Hakar.

General Bits and Pieces

House Darthar.

Jonathon - Othara a'Anathor a'Mdator a'Zgura a'Winfa a'Relda d'Darthar - Head of House Darthar, and Lord of the Darthar family, both branches (Darthar and Darthar Na).

Karanly - Karanalador, first sister. She is the Damadon (sort of an Aunt) to Dee's daughters.

Jant - second brother - cross-tie to Nerela, Head, House Tartarnon.

Silneana - second sister.

Hakar - third brother - aiding Doma..

Rinil - fourth brother.

Aberly - third sister.

Antel - fourth sister.

House Darthar Na.

Dee - Daliera Fontala a'Anathor a'Mdator a'Zgura a'Winfa a'Relda d'Darthar Na. Head of House Darthar Na.

Ar - Ar'ga'da'fazza'din'ban'ahm'na. Dee's Advisor and Teacher.

Tiela - first daughter

Winala - second daughter, The Anointed One.

The House Beasts of Darthar Na.

Kartar - a great grizzly bear looking animal with thick, light green scales. One of them was named Gooda by

Dee when she was a very young child.

The Inferno Hounds - horse sized animals that vaguely look like dogs. The four that are permanent residents of House Darthar Na. Dee named them Manny, Moe, Jack, and Peter.

Furleen - lion sized, cougar looking, feline creatures with bronze colored fur and white tiger stripes on their shoulders and neck. Dee named the one of the house, Purr Cat.

Tarken - giant eagle-like birds who stand taller than most men, the pair are called Hack and Jack by Dee.

Sub-Houses of the Darthar.

suta Namel

suta Ean

suta Zbtan

suta Dundar

suta Milaton

- who gifted the *Hamel*, the Ice Cats.

suta Ocedaron

suta Farbin

Dee's Cousin-Houses and their Heads.

Dalir - Parlente

Namata - Fam

Induna - Armilin, Anointed One.

Patal - deeply hidden, they gave the Word's Ring back to Dee.

Angorson - Pardosh

Anathor - Fraz

The Fontala - Organization.

Daliera Fontala - The Word of The Fontala
Armilin ♀ - The One of The All - House Induna.

First Stand.

Amadur ♂ - First Hand - House Argonar.
Farlon ♂ - The One Who Remembers - House Faradon.

Second Stand

Meludo ♀ - First Hand - House Telat.
Delat ♀ - The One Who Remembers - House Trillmar.

Third Stand

Cantala ♀ - First Hand - House Zbtan.
Trakatar ♂ - The One Who Remembers - House Nerian.

Fourth Stand

Stregt ♂ - First Hand - House Ovever.
Wisuot ♀ - The One Who Remembers - House Zilan.

Fifth Stand

Mensta ♀ - First Hand - House Darunat.
Udoat ♀ - The One Who Remembers - House Hantaz.

Sixth Stand

Oatut ♀ - First Hand - House Quartep-Vierda.
Uztal ♂ - The One Who Remembers - House Abalam.

Seventh Stand

Kitea ♀ - First Hand - House Induna
Anagon ♀ - The One Who Remembers - House Naztan.
Yallan ♂ - The Seeker - House Farback.

♂ = male.
♀ = female.

About the Author

George R. Mead began to study anthropology in 1962 after being discharged (honorably) from the U. S. Army, Combat Engineers. He eventually received his degrees, a B.A., a M. A., and a Ph. D. in his chosen field. And many years later an M. S. W. in Clinical Social Work. He has worked in aerospace, taught at the college and university levels, worked in a community action agency, ran a restaurant, been unemployed, and worked for the U. S. Forest Service. He is now retired from the work-a-day world but does a certain amount of consulting, writing, and research. He lives seven miles outside of the small town of La Grande, Oregon, with his wife, one cat, and one dog. Rez joined the house as an eight-week old puppy found by Katy, a German Shepard (now deceased) under some brush in the middle of the American Southwest desert. Rez is now weighs 107 pounds (some puppy).

www.ingramcontent.com/pod-product-compliance
Lightning Source LLC
Chambersburg PA
CBHW070459260626
47161CB00004B/1380